LETHAL GAME

RED STONE SECURITY SERIES

Katie Reus

Copyright © 2017 by Katie Reus

All rights reserved. Except as permitted under the U.S. Copyright Act of 1976, no part of this publication may be reproduced, distributed, or transmitted in any form or by any means, or stored in a database or retrieval system, without the prior written permission of the author. Thank you for buying an authorized version of this book and complying with copyright laws. You're supporting writers and encouraging creativity.

Cover art: Jaycee of Sweet 'N Spicy Designs
Editor: Julia Ganis
Author website: http://www.katiereus.com

Publisher's Note: This is a work of fiction. Names, characters, places, and incidents are either the products of the author's imagination or used fictitiously, and any resemblance to actual persons, living or dead, or business establishments, organizations or locales is completely coincidental.

Lethal Game/Katie Reus. -- 1st ed.

ISBN-10: 1635560004
ISBN-13: 9781635560008

eISBN: 9781942447962

For Kari Walker. Thank you for being on this wild ride with me since the very first book of the series.

Praise for the novels of Katie Reus

"Sexy military romantic suspense!" —USA Today

"...a wild hot ride for readers. The story grabs you and doesn't let go."
—*New York Times* bestselling author, Cynthia Eden

"Has all the right ingredients: a hot couple, evil villains, and a killer action-filled plot.... [The] Moon Shifter series is what I call Grade-A entertainment!" —Joyfully Reviewed

"I could not put this book down.... Let me be clear that I am not saying that this was a good book *for* a paranormal genre; it was an excellent romance read, *period.*" —All About Romance

"Reus strikes just the right balance of steamy sexual tension and nail-biting action....This romantic thriller reliably hits every note that fans of the genre will expect." —*Publishers Weekly*

"Prepare yourself for the start of a great new series! . . . I'm excited about reading more about this great group of characters."
—Fresh Fiction

"Wow! This powerful, passionate hero sizzles with sheer deliciousness. I loved every sexy twist of this fun & exhilarating tale. Katie Reus delivers!" —Carolyn Crane, RITA award winning author

"You'll fall in love with Katie's heroes."
—*New York Times* bestselling author, Kaylea Cross

"A sexy, well-crafted paranormal romance that succeeds with smart characters and creative world building."—Kirkus Reviews

Continued...

"*Mating Instinct*'s romance is taut and passionate . . . Katie Reus's newest installment in her Moon Shifter series will leave readers breathless!" —Stephanie Tyler, *New York Times* bestselling author

"Exciting in more ways than one, well-paced and smoothly written, I'd recommend *A Covert Affair* to any romantic suspense reader."
—Harlequin Junkie

"*Dangerous Protector* is a suspense filled story of mystery and romance. ... Reus add another wonderful and enthralling installment to her fabulous Red Stone Security romantic suspense series."
—The Reading Café

"If you are looking for a really good, new military romance series, pick up *Targeted*! The new Deadly Ops series stands to be a passionate and action-riddled read."
—That's What I'm Talking About

"Sexy suspense at its finest."
—Laura Wright, *New York Times* bestselling author of *Branded*

"...a captivating, heated, romantic suspense that will pull you in from the beginning and won't let you go until the very last page."
—Amy, So Many Reads

"*Avenger's Heat* hits the ground running and never lets up, whether that be in the action, well-constructed plot or the sexual chemistry between the characters. This is a story of strength, of partnership and healing, and it does it brilliantly." —Vampire Book Club

"*Mating Instinct* was a great read with complex characters, serious political issues and a world I am looking forward to coming back to."
—All Things Urban Fantasy

CHAPTER ONE

Isa looked at her phone screen, pretending to check her email as she waited for her partner to make the drop-off. He was five minutes late.

Which wasn't out of the realm of normalcy for him.

But today was the final day of their job and they were already cutting it close. She had to smuggle the necessary information out and they'd be done. Finally. She liked the temp jobs she took, especially since she got to steal all sorts of interesting stuff, but she was ready to get out of this place. Two weeks was longer than normal for a job.

"Marci," a familiar male voice called out, using her fake name, forcing her to look up. She'd already gone through the body scanner and if her freaking partner would hurry up, she could get the flash drive and be gone. She only had eight more minutes until she had to be out of the building and meet her boss.

She pasted on a pleasant smile even though she knew Brent was going to ask her out. Again. Guy needed to learn to take no for an answer. "Hey, you leaving already?"

He nodded, his smile a little too big. "Yeah, about to grab some drinks for happy hour at Instant Replay. What about you?"

The sports bar was a few blocks away so she wouldn't have to worry about running into him, thankfully. "I'm meeting with friends." She kept her answer as neutral as possible. As far as looks went, the man was attractive. About six feet, dark hair, dark eyes, in good shape, maybe seven or eight years older than her. He was successful too, the VP of one of the marketing departments of the agricultural company. But he was pushy and she didn't like that. Who was she kidding? She didn't want to date anyone right now. Not after the way her heart had been broken a year ago.

"If you want to meet up with me when you're done, I'll be out for a couple hours..." As he continued talking she spotted Antoine, her partner, in her peripheral vision.

He was a new member of the security team at the agricultural company, so he didn't have to go through the scanners. Technically he was *supposed* to, but the security here was lax and the guys who were watching everyone didn't follow all the rules.

It was definitely a problem the company needed to fix. Lucky for her they hadn't yet. But they would after today, she was certain. The owner had hired Red Stone Security—where she *really* worked—to literally steal from them.

Antoine rolled his eyes at Brent's back. Yeah, he didn't like the guy either. Whenever they worked jobs together he was always protective. Actually he was protective of women in general, something she adored about him.

Since Isa and Antoine weren't supposed to know each other she didn't acknowledge him, just moved to the side ever so slightly, giving Antoine his opening. They'd worked together enough that she knew exactly what he would do to get Brent off her back.

In a seemingly clumsy trip, Antoine shoulder-bumped Brent, dropping his coffee onto the floor. The dark liquid spilled on Brent's shoes, creating a pool. "Sorry, man." Antoine's expression was full of remorse as he turned toward Brent.

At the same moment he slid his hand behind his back, handing off the flash drive to Isa with practiced efficiency. He continued with his apology, practically shoving himself in Brent's face and offering to help clean up—giving Isa her escape.

"Gotta run, Brent," she said, her heels clicking across the tile of the lobby floor as she made a beeline for one of the glass doors. Time was ticking down. She and Antoine only got their bonus if she made it to the meeting by or before the deadline.

She heard Brent call out her name, but ignored him as she pushed open the door. A cool rush of air rolled over her. December in Florida was milder than most places but the change in season was much needed from the sweltering summer they'd had.

The neon sign of the sports bar across the busy four-lane street flashed blue and red, advertising happy hour prices. Once there was an opening in traffic she raced across the street. Jaywalking was the least of her crimes today.

As she reached the other sidewalk she could see Harrison Caldwell through one of the huge windows, sitting at a high top table with Kenneth Fairfax, CEO of the company she'd just stolen from.

Harrison glanced at her and raised his eyebrows. No doubt he'd give her grief later about how close she was cutting it.

She just pursed her lips and hurried through the front door. Ignoring the hostess's attempt to seat her, she made her way through the crowd of loud men and women until she reached the window table.

Fairfax startled in his seat to see her. "Ms. Harper."

She nodded once and set the flash drive on the table. "You need to reevaluate your security, Mr. Fairfax."

Frowning, he looked at the small black flash drive. "What is this?"

"Very sensitive information, including new info for a patent on wheat." She might not understand all of the science behind what she'd stolen, but it had been carefully secured in their system. Which meant it was important.

He still hadn't touched it. "You're scanned every day when you leave," he said, his expression disbelieving.

"I am." She tilted her chin at the drive. "See what I left the building with, then let's talk." She nudged Harrison with her elbow. "Forget your manners?"

He just snorted and moved over so she could sit while Fairfax plugged the flash drive into his tablet.

"Cutting it close," Harrison murmured.

She just smiled sweetly. She was on time. That was all that mattered.

He frowned again and she knew he wanted to ask her if Brent had been bothering her, but he wouldn't say anything in front of Fairfax. Harrison could go all protective male sometimes. Something about the men of Red Stone Security—they were all ridiculously alpha.

Harrison always treated her like a kid sister, something she secretly liked since she didn't have any siblings. Harrison and his wife Mara had pretty much taken her under their wing a year ago when she started working for Red Stone, and she adored both of them. Most people at work were scared of Harrison but she didn't understand why. Especially since Isa had seen the way he was with his wife and his nephew. The guy was a giant teddy bear where they were concerned.

She lifted a shoulder while Fairfax clacked away on his tablet. After a long moment, Fairfax cleared his throat, his face pale as he removed the flash drive and tucked it into his pocket.

"I watched you on the security feed today," he said to her, his voice accusing.

"You hired me—us—to show you your company's security flaws. What did you see when you watched me today?" They didn't always tell their clients the day they'd be stealing the info, but sometimes they did to prove a point. Fairfax had been watching her like a hawk via a video feed on his laptop; had even had the security team on high alert today. Not for her specifically, just a general alert. But security hadn't been watching very diligently after people went through their scans. And too bad for him—he hadn't known about her partner. Something he should have thought of.

"You working like normal. You didn't even take a proper lunch break. You didn't take any company property out of the building and even left your cell phone at the main desk when you started work."

"You're right. However, I had a partner. Once I was free of the security scans, I just had to wait for him in the lobby to drop off what I'd already downloaded and stolen first thing this morning. I got in early so I could hack into one of the assistants' computers. I used a manager's code to access the info. From there it was simply a matter of getting it out of the building. I told my partner where the drive would be so he could pick it up. He avoided security because he is part of your security team." So there was no electronic trail either, no real proof that any info had left the building. They never would have known they'd been robbed.

Fairfax's expression went dark and he looked to Harrison for confirmation. "Partner?"

"You contacted me because you wanted to test your security. Don't act surprised that I didn't tell you all the measures we'd be taking. A real thief certainly wouldn't tell you their plans. Her partner is one of my employees and has been working in your security department two weeks longer than Isa. You need stricter security protocols for the actual security department more than anything." Harrison's words were to the point.

"I've already started a list of measures you'll need to take to lock things down more tightly. What you have now isn't bad," Isa said, softening her voice just a fraction. "You just need to strengthen things, that's all. You did the right thing by hiring us."

Fairfax straightened in his chair, nodding more to himself than them. His expression wasn't as grim as it had been. "Well...I must admit I didn't think you'd be able to steal anything this important, but I'd rather know now. Thank you both. If you'll excuse me, I need to make a call."

Isa turned to Harrison as Fairfax slid out of his chair. Once he was out of range she picked up a beer from the ice bucket and tipped it toward Harrison. "To another success."

Half-smiling, he lifted his own beer. "He was so smug before you showed up, so sure you couldn't steal from him."

She snorted. "You look far too happy that we've disappointed him."

"Heck yeah, I am. We just got a sweet bonus and...I have a new job for you. One I think you'll find challenging."

"Yeah?"

"Yep, but no details until tomorrow. I've assigned Antoine to an actual security detail for the next month so you'll be working with a new partner."

She wanted to grill him but knew better. Harrison could be very tight-lipped when he wanted. Since she knew he'd once been a spook, she figured even torture wouldn't get the details out of him. "Fine. Unless you need me for anything else, I'm ready to get out of here."

Shaking his head, he flicked a glance over her shoulder for the briefest of moments. Something strange flashed in his gaze. He looked almost annoyed. She turned around and saw Fairfax on the phone and a bunch of other random people. Nothing looked out of the ordinary.

"What's up?" she asked, turning back to face him, wondering if she should be alarmed about something.

"Nothing. Just tired. Ready to wrap up with him and get out of here." His espresso-colored eyes didn't give away anything.

She slid off her chair, small purse in hand. "Then I'll leave you to it. See you in the morning."

As she skirted her way through the crowd her breath caught in her throat when she saw a familiar face through the group standing near the bar. When she blinked, however, he was gone.

Heart racing out of control, she inwardly cursed herself. Tall, Dark and Stupidly Handsome had never been there at all. What was the matter with her? He would have no business being in Miami—or anywhere in her vicinity.

She hadn't thought about him in...a couple days. Which was a record for her. She'd been so busy working it had been easy enough to forget about the lying sack of shit who'd broken her heart a year ago.

Good thing for him that he wasn't here. Because if he was, she'd have followed through with the violent impulse to punch him in his perfect face.

* * *

"Don't give me that look," Graysen snarled as he slid into the seat across from Harrison. He'd been waiting for that CEO to leave.

Harrison had started to respond when the bartender who'd been serving Graysen earlier approached the table. "You leaving the bar?"

"Yeah, joining a friend." He tried not to snarl at her, since she was just doing her job. "I'll close out my tab." He pulled out a few bills and left them on the table. "Keep the change."

Her eyes widened slightly but she just nodded and pocketed the money—then not so subtly left a piece of paper with her phone number on it in its place. "I get off in an hour."

He didn't respond as she left, but crumpled the paper up once he was sure she wasn't looking and tossed it into the empty ice bucket. He didn't want anyone but Isa.

"What were you thinking, showing up here?" Harrison's voice was razor sharp.

"I had to see her." Graysen knew he'd be meeting with Isa tomorrow, but the urge to get just a glimpse of her again in person was too much. The woman was his obsession. After a year of no contact, no hearing her voice, he was at his breaking point.

Harrison scrubbed a hand over his face, the action out of place on the normally stoic man. "She's going to be pissed tomorrow."

"She'll get over it." Isa had to. She had to forgive him. He couldn't live with anything less. He wouldn't. "And I'm bringing you a huge job." Graysen had gone to Keith Caldwell instead of Harrison, asking Harrison's father— also the founder of Red Stone Security—to hire him now that he'd left the Agency. He was more than qualified, but he didn't just want a *job*. He wanted to specifically work with Isa. So he'd brought an exclusive government contract Red Stone wouldn't want to turn down. It was practically tailored for Isa's expertise. If she was forced to work with Graysen, he could remind her how good they'd been together. And he could work on getting her to forgive him. Which…was the biggest problem.

"Yeah, and you never let me forget it," Harrison muttered.

Graysen lifted a shoulder. He wasn't sorry. He'd do anything to get Isa back. Once she'd left him he'd gone into a downward spiral. After trying to get her to forgive him, apologizing too many times to count only to be shut out, he'd drowned himself in vodka for about a month until he'd realized he was being a giant pussy. He wasn't just going to let her go. So he'd spent the last few months working on getting a huge contract to bring to Red Stone when he left the CIA. It had been a balancing act, getting this contract while still working for the government. But a lot of people owed him favors and he'd cashed in a ton of them. She was that important to him. Hell, she was the most important thing to him.

"If she refuses to work with you—"

"She won't."

Harrison eyed him over the top of his beer, his expression unconvinced. Harrison was a couple years younger than Graysen but he'd been a damn good agent back when they'd been in Black Ops together. They hadn't worked together often, but Harrison was one of the few people Graysen truly respected. The man had a solid code of honor and he was a patriot. Maybe more of a Boy Scout than Graysen, but that wasn't necessarily a bad trait.

Televisions blared inane sports bullshit above them and people were talking and laughing with no concern for anyone around them. Whereas he knew how many people were at the bar right now, the specific layout of the restaurant, how many exits there were—which were closest—and how many people were outside the window. No doubt Harrison could detail all that information as well.

"Mara's pissed about the whole situation," Harrison said.

"You told her?" He snapped out the words louder than he'd planned, but no one around them seemed to notice.

"Yep." No apology from Harrison either.

"Is she going to tell Isa?" Because Harrison had made it clear to Graysen that Isa meant a lot to Mara. And Mara had been a spook too. Graysen wasn't exactly sure which branch but he guessed MI6.

"No, but she wants to."

"After tomorrow it won't matter."

"Look...just don't get your hopes up about this." For the first time since Graysen had known Harrison, the guy actually looked and sounded concerned. For him.

"About what?"

"About Isa. She's never mentioned you, never mentioned an ex, nothing. And what you did was... I don't know if you can come back from that."

Graysen didn't respond, just turned to stare out the window at the passing traffic and the bright lights of downtown Miami. Yeah, he'd screwed up good. That was the understatement of the century.

He'd infiltrated her father's business, lied about who he was, seduced her and broken her heart—and inadvertently gotten her father killed.

If it was the last damn thing he did, he was going to make things right between them.

CHAPTER TWO

Did you do what I told you to?
Isa shook her head as she read Mara's text, a smile tugging at her lips. A man stepped up next to her, joining the crowd of people waiting for the elevator.

Her fingers flew across the screen. *Yes, weirdo. You're the only woman I know who would order me to dress sexy when going to a meeting with said woman's own husband.*

Mara had called her this morning and ordered her to wear something designed to make a man's tongue fall out of his mouth. She hadn't actually done what Mara had said because this was a professional environment, but she'd dressed up a little more than normal.

You'll thank me later, came Mara's responding text.

Is this about who I'm meeting with today? You know I don't mix business and pleasure. So even if her new partner was sexy as sin it wouldn't matter. He might as well be sexless. She didn't have any interest in anyone, anyway. Not since... She swallowed hard, shutting that thought down.

"You look really familiar," the man next to her said.

Since Mara hadn't responded Isa tucked her phone into her purse and gave the man a neutral smile. When she looked at him, however, she realized she had seen him somewhere. The memory of that 'meeting' was disgusting. "I don't think so," she murmured. Yeah, she really didn't want to talk to *this* guy.

"No, I'm really good with faces and I'm certain we've met before." He watched her carefully, looking at her as if he was trying to decide if he'd seen her naked or not.

The guy's whole demeanor was off-putting and she wondered if he was a new client for Red Stone. She certainly hoped not. "The reason I probably look familiar," she said quietly, dropping her voice so that the others around them couldn't hear, "is because I was at Club Bardot the other night and saw a prostitute give you a blow job right in the VIP section." She'd been there following someone for one of her past jobs—seeing if there was another angle to being able to infiltrate the company. Meaning, potential bribery of an employee. She hadn't had to use that angle, thankfully.

He blinked in clear surprise, but he didn't seem embarrassed. "She wasn't a prostitute."

That was his response? She coughed to cover up an uncomfortable laugh. "Oh, I just assumed."

He straightened, clearly not deterred. "Well, listen—"

She shook her head. "I'm not trying to be rude, but I literally had to see your dick against my will when you whipped it out for the entire VIP section to see. I don't think we have anything to say to each other."

Isa heard a woman snicker behind her and realized she hadn't been as quiet as she'd thought. But seriously, it was too early in the morning for this. She hadn't even had her coffee yet.

The guy shrugged, not even fazed. "Your loss."

She snorted to herself. Yeah, she was sure she'd lose a lot of sleep over this guy. When two elevators' doors opened, she slipped into the opposite one he got into. At thirty she was too young to be out of the dating game, but damn, if this was what was out there, she was fine being single. She hadn't been in any state of mind to start dating again over the last year, and right about now she was glad for that.

As people streamed into the elevator, her phone dinged a few times in a row. Scrolling through her messages, all from work, she started responding as the car whooshed to life. A few people quietly talked amongst themselves but one by one everyone disembarked as the elevator rose higher and higher. Normally she made an effort to talk to people and be polite but this morning she didn't have it in her.

After leaving the restaurant yesterday evening she'd been feeling off. She knew why, too. She'd thought of Graysen West all night. Had even dreamed of him. It was making her edgy, and she hated that—but she didn't hate him. That was what drove her the craziest. She should hate the man after what he'd done, but...some stupid part of her still held on to all those sweet memories.

Lies, she reminded herself. All those memories might be real but everything about them had been a lie. *Ugh, get the freak over it already.* She wished life was that easy, that she could just order herself to forget him and move on. Unfortunately, getting over a man like Graysen was hard. It wasn't just that he was sexy—which he was. He was giving and sweet... *Gah,* and a giant liar. What the hell was wrong with her? He wasn't giving or sweet. He sucked.

As a woman moved off past her, Isa slipped her phone into her jacket pocket and glanced at the shiny chrome keypad on the elevator wall. Only three floors to go. She hadn't dressed as sexy as Mara had said to, but she was wearing a dark green sheath dress with high heels that she could admit showed off her toned calves. She didn't love everything about her body—what woman did?—but she liked her legs.

"You really need better spatial awareness." A familiar, deep voice from behind her made her jump out of her skin.

Feeling almost numb, she turned to find Graysen West standing there—and looking way too sexy for his own good. Or for *her* own good. She'd thought she was completely alone in the elevator now.

She blinked once. Yep, he was still there. Well over six feet of raw masculinity, bright blue eyes she could drown in, and a disapproving frown that somehow made him look sexy.

"When did you get on?" Okay, that was probably the dumbest thing that could have come out of her mouth, but whatever. She was just glad she'd found her voice.

"Same time you did. But you were too busy on your phone to notice." He frowned, looking all judgmental, and she just about snapped.

"Seriously, that's the first thing you say to me? You criticize me about being on my phone?" She'd been working, not that that was remotely the point. He had no say in her life. If she wanted to play games on her phone, she damn well would.

"You've got to pay better attention to your surroundings. Did you even know there was someone else still on the elevator with you?"

Isa felt almost possessed as she lashed out. A year of built-up anger and hurt came bursting to the surface with his obnoxious 'I know better than you' tone. Her arm was moving before she'd processed what she was doing but when her fist connected with his nose, she cursed at the pain that jolted through her hand. Punching someone *hurt*.

He grunted as his head snapped back. But other than that he barely reacted.

She belatedly realized he hadn't even moved to defend himself, and considering his training, he would have with anyone else. Stupid tears stung her eyes because she felt bad for punching him and she hated the insane way she'd just reacted to seeing him. It was completely nuts. She'd literally just assaulted someone in an elevator.

But Graysen apparently brought out the crazy in her. She spun away from him as the elevator doors opened, glad that no one was waiting and thankful for the escape. She didn't care why he was here. She wasn't dealing with him right now. Not now, not ever.

She heard him call her name but she ignored him and ducked in to the nearest women's bathroom before he could see her cry. She'd cried enough over that man and she'd punch him again before she let him see her have an emotional breakdown.

* * *

Fuck, fuck, fuck.

Holding a hand to his bleeding nose, Graysen started to follow after Isa but held back. He'd already screwed up by surprising her in the elevator.

He'd been staring at her perfect ass the last couple minutes and she hadn't had a clue he'd been there.

What if some nut had been in the elevator with her? God, how many times had he told her to pay better attention... He inwardly cursed. Yeah, not the point right now. *Not the point at all.*

Turning away from the closed bathroom door, he headed down the quiet hallway. He didn't want to leave her, but he thought he'd seen tears glistening in her eyes before she stormed off. He didn't want to ambush her again. Not when he knew she needed time to compose herself.

As he moved toward Harrison's office he quickly catalogued his surroundings as he always did. Everything was decorated in soft blues and greens, and Van Gogh prints lined the main hallway. Graysen knew that Harrison headed up a few departments, including the new one that Isa had been working with the last year.

When he stepped into Harrison's assistant's space, the dark-haired woman's eyes widened. She started to stand. "Mr. West—"

He shook his head. "I'm fine."

She eyed him warily but nodded. "Okay... Mr. Caldwell is in his office. He said to send you in when you arrived. Ms. Harper isn't here yet but I expect her any moment. She's always on time." As she spoke she was already buzzing Harrison to let him know that Graysen was here.

Graysen only entered when she gave him the go-ahead. Harrison didn't look exactly surprised when he saw Graysen standing there bleeding.

Harrison rounded his desk and headed to the small bar near the big spread of windows that overlooked the city. With efficient movements, he filled a small plastic bag with ice from the minibar and pulled out a pack of wet wipes. He handed them to Graysen before sitting back down.

"Got a call from security," Harrison said mildly as Graysen started cleaning up the blood. There wasn't much, but his nose still hurt.

Crap. Of course security would have seen Isa punch him. "What did you tell them?"

"To let me deal with it. Damn it, Graysen. Isa is normally one of the calmest, most rational people I know. It's why she fits so well with this new venture Red Stone has taken on. We're appreciative of the new contract you've brought us, but did you ever stop to wonder if you're going to screw up her work dynamic?"

Yeah, he'd thought of it. But this was the only way he could get her to talk to him, to interact with him. She'd shut him down every other time he'd tried to reach out to her—not that he blamed her. "Just give me a chance. This one job with her." The job he'd managed to snag was huge. Raptor Aeronautical—an aeronautical engineering company that took on contract government jobs designing military aircraft. The CEO wanted to tighten things up and do an annual check on security, and Graysen had convinced him to hire Red Stone for the check. They'd just been waiting on the final approval. "One week working with her, and if she wants, I'll step back. You can replace me with someone else." Even saying those words made him break out in a cold sweat. He wasn't sure that he could convince Isa after only a week but he was damn sure going to try.

"Is that a promise?" Isa's quiet voice made him turn in his seat.

Emerald green eyes frosty, her expression was just as icy. All her muscles were pulled taut and her shoulders were stiff as she stepped through the open doorway.

Guess she wasn't the only one who needed to increase their spatial awareness.

He met her gaze, aware of the way his heart pounded. "Work with me one week, once this contract starts. And if it's too much I promise never to bother you again." *Liar, liar*, the little voice in his head said. He wasn't sure he could walk away from her.

She didn't say anything to him, just looked at Harrison in confusion and a little hurt.

The hurt clawed at Graysen. Suddenly his big plan seemed stupid.

"Shut the door," Harrison said quietly.

Once Isa did, he motioned to the seat next to Graysen.

She glided toward him and sat ramrod straight. She'd pulled her long, dark hair into a twist at her neck. Not one perfect hair was out of place. Petite with the right amount of curves, Isa was the only woman who'd ever gotten to him. And then he'd broken her trust and her heart and screwed everything up completely.

"I should have told you Mr. West was going to be your new partner." Harrison's voice was sincere as he looked at Isa. "I'm sorry for ambushing you."

"So you know...about our history?"

Harrison nodded once. "I used to work with Graysen and he recently approached me about a new job."

"Oh." She bit her bottom lip, looking vulnerable.

Graysen had the sudden urge to take that bottom lip between his teeth, nibble on it and her. God he missed her. Had missed her every day and night since she'd left him. Even if it was his own fault.

"Graysen is our newest employee."

Those beautiful green eyes widened just a bit as she finally turned to face him. "You're not with the CIA anymore?"

He shook his head, not trusting his voice and not trusting himself not to say something else stupid.

"He brought a big contract with him as part of his hiring, but it's been top secret until this morning. Still is, if you want to get technical," Harrison said. "It's why I couldn't say anything to you. Not until you'd been approved by the CEO for the job. You've got the clearance for it and so does Graysen, but the CEO still had final approval, and he needed to finish reviewing your file and work history. Hands down, I think you're the best fit for this job. It's a huge deal for Red Stone. I just need to know that you'll be able to work with him."

She was quiet for a long moment and Graysen could practically see the gears turning in her sexy head. Before Red Stone she'd worked for a company that had analyzed other companies' work effectiveness. Often for government facilities. She'd always had a high level of clearance and she was one of the most capable women he knew. It was one of the reasons he liked her so much.

Once things had blown up between them, however, she'd quit her job in DC and moved to Miami to start fresh, away from him and her memories.

"I will be a professional," she finally said.

Graysen noticed the way she subtly flexed her fingers, and handed her the small pack of ice.

It seemed as if she wanted to protest but she took it and murmured, "Thank you."

As long as she wasn't punching him, he'd take it.

Standing, Harrison cleared his throat. "I need to grab a few more items for this meeting. I'll be back in a couple minutes."

Graysen knew that was utter bullshit but figured Harrison wanted to give them time alone.

When the door closed behind him Isa turned toward Graysen. "How's your nose?" Her tone was pointed, her expression making it clear she thought he deserved the pain.

"Not broken." He drank in the sight of her, unable to get enough. Looking at a picture of her wasn't the same as seeing her in person. The elegant line of her neck, the sweet curves of her breasts under her dress—which he shouldn't be noticing right now.

"I...should probably apologize, but I'm not exactly sorry." Guilt flickered in her eyes.

Which made him adore her even more. She felt bad for *not* being sorry. "I deserved it."

She rubbed an unsteady hand over her face. "Jeez, Graysen, what the heck are you doing here? Did you..." She cleared her throat. "I thought you loved your job." There was a hint of bitterness in the last few words and he understood it.

She thought he'd chosen his job over her, over his love for her. He loved her a lot more than a job, but he held back. That definitely wasn't the way to get to her and she wouldn't believe him now anyway. "I'd never planned to stay with the Agency forever. Red Stone is a good company."

"I...hope you didn't get this job in a misguided effort to, uh, win me back." Her cheeks flushed slightly. "Because that's never happening. We're done."

He decided to ignore her words for now. Because he didn't want to lie to her. He'd lied to her enough. Telling her the flat-out truth probably wasn't the way to go either. Telling her that hell yeah, he'd gotten this job for her wouldn't do him any favors at the moment. "I go way back with Harrison. Keith Caldwell too. I'd always talked about working here once I retired." Of course he'd been a couple decades away from retiring. "Some stuff happened at work recently and that timeline got moved up."

"Oh." She seemed relieved by that. "Well...it's a shock seeing you." She let out a nervous laugh and gestured to her iced hand. "Obviously. But I promise no more outbursts of violence. Unless provoked."

He'd have given anything to be able to take her hand in his, stroke his thumb over it, try to ease her pain. Pain he'd caused her yet again. "How's your hand?"

"Okay. I've never punched anyone before." She let out another one of those nervous laughs as her cheeks flushed again.

He hated being the cause of her discomfort. "Well, you're good at it."

She gave him a real laugh and rolled her eyes. "That's a strange compliment."

Before he could respond Harrison strode back in, his expression all business. Time to get down to work.

Even if that was the last thing he wanted to do. But he had to play this right, to be professional and show Isa how good things could be between them. Show her that he still loved her—and that he would never hurt her again.

Because in his end game, Isa was the woman he wanted to spend the rest of his life with. Even if he didn't deserve her, he'd damn sure spend the rest of his life making her happy.

CHAPTER THREE

I'm going to kill you Isa texted to Mara as she headed down in the elevator to her office.

I think you mean thank me. Otherwise you wouldn't have gotten all sexy today. How's your hand feel?

How do you even know about that? Isa hadn't left Harrison's office until a few minutes ago.

I have my ways.

I can actually hear you cackling as you say that. Ugh, my hand is fine. I'm a little embarrassed though.

From what I hear, he deserved more than a punch.

Isa had never told Mara about Graysen. Not specifically, anyway. When she'd become friends with Mara, Isa had mentioned an ex who was a liar, but that had been the extent of things. Talking about Graysen had just been too hard and she didn't like people knowing all her business. But if Harrison knew about Isa and Graysen's history, then no doubt Mara knew everything too. Still, Isa didn't feel like talking about it now. She just wanted to hide out in her office and lick her wounds and pretend that when the new contract started in two weeks she wouldn't be working with her ex-boyfriend— for one stupid week.

Probably, she texted back.

She tucked her phone into her purse when she reached her floor. And when she made it to her office and found Lizzy Caldwell sitting in the chair in front of the desk, offering up a cappuccino, she almost burst into tears. "That's for me?"

Lizzy grinned. "Yep, just the way you like it. I added two sugars."

"I freaking love you."

"I know. I'm very loveable." Lizzy kicked her feet out in front of her and Isa saw that she was wearing purple and pink Chuck Taylors. She had on jeans and a T-shirt that said *Nerd? I prefer the term Intellectual Badass.* The shirt made Isa grin. Lizzy didn't care about 'being professional' at the office. Probably because she was headhunted by government agencies all the time and knew how invaluable she was to the company. It didn't hurt that she was married to one of the owners, either.

"Not that I don't appreciate this," Isa said, holding up her drink as she sat. "Or the company. But what are you doing in my neck of the woods?" Their offices were actually on the same floor, but they didn't work together often.

Lizzy shrugged, a mischievous grin on her face. "Just knew you'd be back in the office today and wanted to say hi. And...I heard you punched a guy and wanted to ask why."

"Oh crap. Does everyone know?" Isa had worked so hard to fit in here. After escaping DC and the hellish stories—truth—of her father being a traitor, she made a point to be a professional at all times. She was sure some people knew about her past, though no one had ever called her on it. Which was fine by her. She didn't want to talk about that with anyone.

Lizzy snorted. "I don't think anyone does, really. I just heard from Porter—who heard from one of the guys in the security room. They let Harrison, Porter and Grant know as standard procedure. Said you have a nice right hook, *chica*."

"It's the first time I've ever punched someone." She took a sip of her cappuccino, grateful for the comfort drink. Her hand was tender but didn't bother her as much as it had a while ago.

"Well why'd you do it?"

"He deserved it."

"Don't be obnoxious."

"I really don't want to talk about it. Not now, anyway. Harrison just gave me a new job and I've got to start prepping for it." Which meant reading over a bunch of files and learning about her 'new colleagues' before she started with them. That was just the tip of the iceberg of what she had to do for her prep.

"Okay, but if you change your mind, just call me. And not because I want gossip—though I always do. And seriously, if you want me to mess up this guy's life, just let me know." She got a wicked glint in her eyes that Isa knew too well. Lizzy really could be scary when she wanted to.

"He's a Red Stone employee."

Lizzy's eyebrows raised. "Porter left that part out."

Isa lifted a shoulder. "He's my new partner for my next job, so please don't screw up his life."

"You're really not making me want to know about him any less, but if you don't want to talk about him, I get it." She stood, pushing the chair back. "I'm here if you need me."

"Thanks, I appreciate it." Once Lizzy was gone Isa set her mug down on her desk and groaned to herself.

She was going to be working a job with sexy, frustrating Graysen West. How the heck had this even happened? Seeing him in that elevator and then in the office had jolted her back to over a year ago, to the first time they'd met. The first time he'd introduced himself and acted as if he had no idea who she was.

As if he hadn't targeted her for a specific reason.

She looked at her cappuccino and frowned, pushing back all sorts of unwanted memories. If she ever had a reason to start day drinking, now was it.

She was too much of a professional to do that though. Or she hoped she was. Because a mimosa—or three—at lunch today sounded like a good freaking idea.

CHAPTER FOUR

Fourteen months ago

"I think this is yours."

The deep, male voice made Isa turn around and look up, up, up into arresting blue eyes.

"What?" She couldn't tear her gaze away from the stranger in front of her. Didn't want to, if she got to look at this eye candy.

"The coffee. I think I grabbed yours by mistake." That deep voice wrapped around her, his mere presence making everything else in the small coffee shop fade away.

Blinking, she looked at the cup he extended then looked at the one in her hand. She turned it and saw the name Michael scribbled in purple ink. She frowned at herself, surprised she'd taken the wrong cup, but held it out to him as he traded with her. "Sorry about that."

"No worries." His smile was easy, those eyes ridiculously gorgeous, and he looked a little out of place in this coffee shop that attracted mostly corporate types.

He had on jeans, a thick Columbia jacket and heavy boots. He topped off the sexy look with a hint of a beard—probably five or so days' worth of dark scruff—and he looked a bit like a lumberjack. Or a ski instructor.

Whatever the look was called, he was walking sex appeal.

She smiled again and was starting to leave when he held out a hand. "I'm Michael."

Stopping, she shook with him. "Ah, Isa."

"Nice to meet you." When her fingers touched his she swore she felt an electric spark travel up her arm. Which was stupid, like something out of a clichéd romantic comedy, but she didn't care.

"You too."

"I was about to head across the street to the park to take my dog for a walk." He motioned to the little gray and white fluffy dog secured outside, looking in the window, watching its master patiently and adoringly. "Want to join me?"

Isa needed to get back to work, but... "Okay." She hadn't been on a date in a while. Mainly because work was insane. And fate decided to drop this guy right in front of her? Yeah, she'd be an idiot to say no.

* * *

Shaking herself out of the buried memory, Isa glanced up from her temporary desk, expecting to see Hamilton Ridler, the CEO of Raptor Aeronautical, since it was Monday, the first day of her temporary job.

Instead it was Graysen, looking good enough to eat in a charcoal suit and a pale grayish-blue tie. It didn't matter what the man wore—he always looked good. Something he knew and used to the best of his advantage. They hadn't talked much in the last two weeks, and for that she was grateful. Now she only had one week to get through and she could tell Harrison she didn't want to work with Graysen anymore.

He'd been here the whole time, working with Mr. Ridler as a new employee—one Ridler was supposedly personally grooming for a high management position. Graysen had been brought in early, and because of his new "position" he had the highest security clearance.

As did she. But she didn't have to lie to the people she was working with about her temporary job. Not really. She'd been hired as a special analyst to see where the company could make some cuts. So of course everyone was terrified of her reporting to the big boss that their job was unnecessary. It also meant people avoided her, which was a good thing. She could do her work in peace, and mostly avoid Graysen in the process.

"Hi, Mr. Evans," she said, using his alias for this job. For the next couple weeks, he was Garret Evans. She got to keep her first name; they'd just changed her last name.

"Isa." He nodded once, his look smoldering as he leaned against the doorframe, not bothering to hide all that heat and hunger.

Gah, why couldn't he keep that stuff to himself? She didn't want to know how much he still wanted her. "Can I help you with something?"

He blinked, as if coming out of a trance. "Yes. I wanted to see if you'd have lunch with me today. You haven't left your office all day."

Frowning, she looked at the clock on her laptop and was surprised to see it was already one o'clock. "I'm not really hungry." She could get like that when on a job—everything but her work took a back seat.

"I insist," he murmured, stepping into the small office that consisted of a desk and an empty bookcase. At least it had a window, but other than that it was bare. There was something in his tone that made her straighten, however.

She stood and started to pick up her laptop but he gave a subtle shake of his head.

She picked up her purse instead, and even though she had questions, she didn't bother asking. She would wait until they were alone.

Once they were in the hall he placed his hand on the small of her back, the action not exactly intimate but it somehow felt like it. "Thanks for taking this tour with me." When he spoke it was a little too loud.

She quickly realized that it was because he *wanted* people to overhear him. He continued talking about the company and how even though he was new, that he and Mr. Ridler were going to make sure Raptor was running as smoothly as it could.

When they reached the elevators she started to ask him why he'd wanted her to leave her laptop but he shook his head again and casually scratched his ear. *Oh, right, someone might be listening in the elevator.* In past jobs that had never been an issue. She'd usually worked with Antoine, but they almost never had any interaction except right until the last day of a job. And even then their contact was covert.

A couple floors later Graysen steered her into what turned out to be a private, windowless office set up with multiple video feeds—including one of her office.

She turned to him, wide-eyed. "You're watching me?" She couldn't believe he hadn't told her. Or that she hadn't noticed a video camera.

He nodded and motioned to the desk with two takeout boxes. "I got you a spicy tuna roll and an edamame salad for our lunch date."

She shouldn't be surprised he remembered that was her favorite. "Thanks...but what is all this?"

"We're staking out your office for the next hour."

She snorted and took a seat in the surprisingly comfortable chair in front of her takeout box. It was cushioned and had a remote control to adjust the back setting as well as a heater for her butt. It had to be a couple grand, easy. "Where'd you get this seat?" she asked as he sat next to her in a normal-looking chair.

He shrugged as he adjusted one of the screens. "It was already in here... No one should bother us on this floor. It's where we'll set up our base of operations."

But there was something in his tone that said it hadn't been and she couldn't help but wonder if he'd gotten it for her. She didn't ask because she didn't want the answer. "So, we're staking out my office. Why didn't you tell me before you had it wired?"

"I knew you'd act weird if you knew I had a camera on you."

Well, that was true. "Okay, fair enough. So...this is a little different from what Antoine and I normally do for our jobs. I didn't think you and I would have much contact."

"As of this morning, Ridler told me that he's certain someone is stealing from the company. Funds from two accounts have gone missing in the last twelve hours. Both over a hundred grand. He's got one of his tech guys on it too, but because of the nature of this breach no one else knows about this."

She opened her lunch and smiled at the spicy scent. "And you think what, someone's going to try to hack my computer?"

He shrugged again, slanting her a glance that reminded her of how he'd looked at her in bed on more than one occasion. She wasn't sure what it was, but something in his expression triggered naked memories. She swallowed hard and focused on the screens. The other feeds displayed the hallway outside her office and what appeared to be a couple of stairwells.

"Can I say something not related to this job?" His voice was low, almost hesitant.

Which was so very unlike him. He was always confident. She tensed. "Sure." She kept her tone as light as she could, even though she knew he was going to talk about them, their past. Now wasn't the time. But the truth was, there was never going to be a good time.

"I know I've said I'm sorry but I'm going to say it again. Did I target you? Yes. Did I plan to sleep with you? No. Fuck. *No.* I'd just planned to meet you and get an invite to your father's estate. That was it." His tone grew harsher, his voice thicker as he continued.

Against her will she turned to him. She didn't want to see his face, didn't want to see any emotions there. For the last year she'd done a good job of locking up all memories of Graysen West into a tiny box in her head.

He looked...vulnerable, his expression so open her breath caught. "Then why did you fuck me?"

He flinched at her harsh wording. "It was more than that."

"Maybe so, but I just...don't even know you. I feel like the man I slept with, told secrets to, doesn't exist. You even lied about your freaking dog too. I opened myself up to a man named *Michael.* So whatever you think you feel for me, I don't feel for you. I felt all those things for him. And he was a lie. And it freaking hurts, Graysen."

"I'm sorry. I know it's hollow and useless, but I am. I wish I could go back. I want...a second chance, Isa. I know I don't deserve it, but I—"

She shook her head, unable to let him continue. "No. There will be no second chance. No chance between us, ever."

He nodded once, swallowing hard. "Is it because of...your father?"

God, she didn't want to talk about her father. She still hadn't come to terms with the man her father had been, all the lies he'd told everyone. He'd been selling state secrets to *terrorists.* "I understand why you and your people went after him and...I believe he wanted to die in that gunfight."

It had been a 'suicide by cop' type of situation, only in her father's case he'd opened fire on FBI agents who'd been working with Graysen's covert CIA team. The FBI had taken him out with little effort.

"That's not why. I can never trust you now. Simple as that." He looked so damn broken she found herself continuing even though it went against all her self-preservation instincts. She knew from experience that he was a good actor. Still, he'd gone to a lot of trouble to work with her. "We can be civil. If you're working for Red Stone, I don't want to be enemies or anything. So, yeah, we can be friendly. That's it though." It took work to say the words.

His blue eyes went shuttered as he nodded. "Okay. Fair warning. I want more. Always will."

"Graysen—"

He stiffened, his gaze darting to one of the screens. She followed where he looked and her eyes widened.

A woman in her mid-forties wearing a navy blue dress went to the window in Isa's office and leaned against it, looking out at the skyline, her body language casual as she started to slowly do a visual scan of the office. It wasn't overt; her moves were very relaxed. Her gaze skimmed right over where the camera must be.

"You really must have hidden that camera well," Isa murmured, watching as the woman quickly went to the laptop and clicked on the keyboard.

Graysen grunted, his gaze intent on the woman for a second, as if memorizing her face. "Gina Scott."

Isa blinked in surprise. "You know her?"

"Not personally. I just memorized the names and faces of anyone who had access to the funds missing."

"That's like...over a hundred people."

He shrugged, as if memorizing that many names and faces wasn't a big deal. She knew he had a good memory, but that was a lot of information to retain. He slid a laptop in front of him, and, fingers flying across the keyboard, pulled up a program she recognized well. Working quickly, he shadowed what the woman was doing so they saw what she saw, but on their own screen—and Gina Scott was completely unaware of their presence. The spyware program was incredible.

Isa frowned. "It looks like she's pulling up different personnel files."

Graysen's frown matched her own. "She's copying them to a flash drive."

Isa pulled out her cell phone and called Emerson Lincoln, a computer programmer/analyst who worked for Red Stone Security. Emerson had been assigned as their backup to run checks on people and handle various research that would save them valuable time. Isa had been working with the sweet woman for about eight months and she was very good at what she did.

Emerson picked up on the second ring. "Hey, girl. How's the job going?"

"Potentially we might have something good for you. Can you do a detailed run on Gina Scott?"

"No problem. Anything specific I should look for?"

"Just the usual stuff," Isa said, even as she took over one of the other laptops, pulling up a file on Gina Scott. "I'm going to review her employee records, but look up all of her financials." It was usually a good place to start with anyone. If someone had new, offshore bank accounts or unexpectedly large deposits into their current one, that was a pretty good sign they were up to no good. Usually people weren't so sloppy, however—Isa wished her job was that easy. But she never knew. If someone didn't realize they were being watched they could get arrogant and sloppy.

As they disconnected Isa watched the woman pull her flash drive out of the computer and tuck it into a slim pocket of her dress. She couldn't even see a tiny bulge giving away the flash drive.

"What did she take?" she asked Graysen.

"It looks as if she just copied financials of other employees. Basically information pertaining to what their annual salaries are."

Isa lifted an eyebrow. "Could just be nosiness."

"Maybe." But Graysen shook his head. "That was a ballsy move."

"Yeah, she moved like a pro, too. Almost like she's done this before." Isa continued scanning Scott's personnel file, noted that the woman had a high-level position in one of the design departments.

"I'm sure Emerson will have something for us soon," Graysen said, speaking about Emerson as if he knew her.

Which for some reason grated on Isa's nerves. Not because she thought he had a chance with the other woman—no, Emerson was smitten with a local detective—but because she'd come to think of Red Stone Security as her home, her people. It was weird to be working with Graysen, for multiple reasons. Because he'd said that he'd bow out of this job after a week if it became too uncomfortable for her. But he hadn't said he'd stop working for Red Stone.

She wasn't sure how she felt about that. About any of this. Because just being in the same room with him, breathing in his addictive, subtle masculine scent, made her a little bit crazy.

"I kept the dog," he said abruptly. Graysen didn't look at her as he focused on the display of video screens, scanning the various secret feeds he'd set up. She wasn't certain where some of the feeds were coming from.

Isa blinked, taking a second to digest his words. He couldn't mean... "Peaches?"

He nodded. "Yeah. She grew on me. She misses you, so if you ever want to stop by and see her, you're welcome to."

She blinked again. "Seriously? You're stooping to using a dog to get in my good graces?"

Graysen's lips perked up the slightest bit. He was clearly unapologetic. "I'll use anything I can to get into your good graces. Including a sweet, adorable dog who would love nothing more than to see you. But I'm not lying. She's currently with her dog sitter, probably soaking up sun on the beach or at the park."

Isa looked away from him. Why the hell had he told her that? She'd loved that little mutt, Peaches. The little girl was a mix of who knew how many breeds, with gray and white fur, floppy ears, and weighed maybe ten pounds soaking wet. And Graysen had kept her?

She knew that the dog was originally part of his cover. He'd admitted as much after his operation blew up in his face. She couldn't believe he'd kept Peaches. It was so obvious what he was trying to do—getting her to come over to his place and see his dog. A dog that she had dearly loved.

He was being so honest and blatant about what he wanted from her and she wasn't sure how to deal with it. After the way he lied to her, betrayed her, being around him again in a new atmosphere had completely rocked her world on its axis. For all she knew, he was lying to get something else from her. Even as she had the thought, she simply couldn't imagine what it would be, what he could hope to gain. He worked for Red Stone now. Had pulled strings to get this job, from all accounts. Just so he could work with her.

She just wanted to get through this job and put some space between them. Only one week, she reminded herself. Maybe then her life would go back to normal. She nearly snorted at the lie she tried to tell herself. Now that Graysen West was back in her life again, she knew things would never be normal again.

CHAPTER FIVE

Alan Persky watched on the video feed from the company's security room as the pretty, dark-haired woman entered the lobby. It was the end of the day and the woman, Isa Johnson, was here at the behest of Hamilton. Hiring that bitch should have gone through him as well, but no one had mentioned it to Alan.

Hamilton could do what he wanted, he always did, but bringing someone in to "trim the fat," especially someone who had the right kind of security clearance to work at this firm, even temporarily, was something Alan should have been informed about.

But Hamilton had been acting strange lately, almost secretive. Which wasn't out of the realm of normalcy, but Hamilton never acted that way with him. Right now there was too much on the line to question the CEO, however.

Frowning, he watched as she exited the building. Her name was so common—Johnson. There were a billion Johnsons in the world. He'd already downloaded her resume and other necessary hiring files and planned to follow up on her, but he wished she wasn't here at all.

Alan didn't need somebody nosing around in any work files right now. Not when he was so close to finishing what he needed to, cashing out and leaving the country for good with the woman he loved. He'd fake his own death as well, but later, once he was long gone. There was the slimmest of chances that Johnson would find what he'd done and he couldn't risk her stumbling upon it.

He could just kill her or have one of his men kill her, but that wouldn't solve anything. It would only draw more attention to the company and his boss would just hire somebody new anyway. No, Alan would just keep an eye on her and make sure she didn't get into anything she shouldn't.

If she did, then she'd have to die.

The other new hire was the one who had him really worried: Garret Evans. There was something about Evans that bothered him on a bone-deep level, but he wasn't certain what it was. All he knew was that he didn't trust the guy. Hamilton had recently hired Evans as well, without running it by him first.

Alan had contemplated that Hamilton might know what he was up to, but if the old man did, Alan would already be in jail and facing charges of treason. If that ever happened, they'd throw him into a dark hole and never let him out. A dark shiver of fear snaked down his spine at the thought of getting caught.

No, he was just being paranoid because of everything on the line. They were getting close to the end of this job and he was letting his fear get the best of him.

Still, it never hurt to be careful. Not with so much at stake.

When the door behind him opened he half turned and nodded politely at one of the security guys coming back from a smoke break. He'd stopped by under the guise of an impromptu visit—as was typical of him to do. Considering his security clearance, when he offered to watch the feeds for a few minutes so the security guy could smoke, the twenty-something man had jumped at the chance. It was against protocol, but when *he* bent the rules people were usually okay with it. That was one of the benefits of his position with the company.

"Nothing unusual," he murmured to the guy before stepping back out into the hall.

He smiled to himself once he was alone. In just a week he would be out of the country, millions of dollars richer, and away from his bullshit, boring life. He was going to leave everything behind him—his debts, his stupid ex-wife, everything. His new fiancée got him like no one else did. She was beautiful, smart and supported him. She wanted to leave the country too. Was so taken with him that she'd go anywhere with him.

Starting fresh was what he needed. Hell, what he deserved. He'd given everything to this company, and yeah, he made decent money. But he could be making more. He should be making more.

At the thought of all the money he'd have soon, some of the earlier fear faded away.

Only a week to go. He still had a couple more things to finish to complete his mission, and then he was home free.

And he'd be incredibly rich. If anyone got in his way, they would simply have to die. Because failure wasn't an option for this. He'd already committed and would see this through until the end.

CHAPTER SIX

"I'm going to need clearance to get into Red Stone tonight," Carlito said into his phone. His former partner and best friend worked there—was one of the co-owners.

"That's your greeting?" Grant Caldwell's voice was dry.

Carlito scrubbed a hand over his face as he headed down the sidewalk in the now quiet business district of downtown Miami. During the daytime it was bustling, but after five or six o'clock it was a ghost town. Tonight it was ice cold, especially for Florida, but it was close to Christmas and while it wouldn't be a white one, they were getting some serious chill. "Sorry, man. How's Belle?" Grant's wife was nine months pregnant and close to popping. They'd already had a few false alarms and rushed to the hospital but as far as Carlito knew, they were back home now.

"We're doing good, she's just tired and cranky. And I can't blame her." Grant sounded exhausted.

Carlito couldn't actually see Belle being cranky—the woman was like a ray of sunshine. She'd been through hell after being kidnapped by a psychotic serial killer, *and* she'd married his grumpy former partner, so she was a saint as far as he was concerned. "Any more false alarms?"

"No. And I hope after the next trip we take to the hospital, we come home with a healthy baby."

"Her family's going to descend on you guys like locusts." Belle's Greek family was huge and…wonderful. They'd pretty much adopted Carlito because of his close relationship with Grant, and he loved them. And Belle's mom was always hinting that she'd love to set him up with one of her nieces. But Carlito only had eyes for one woman, hence the call to Grant tonight.

Grant let out a short, tired laugh. "They already have. They've been dropping off tons of casseroles. We've frozen most of them. The food has been amazing so I can't complain too much. So what's up? Why do you need to get into the building?"

"You know exactly why," he gritted out.

"I know, I just want to hear you say it."

"Emerson is working late, and I want to bring her dinner." Emerson Lincoln, the woman he planned to marry one day. If only he could ever get her to see him as something other than a friend.

Grant laughed again. "You are so gone over her."

Yeah, no shit. "You really gonna give me grief tonight?" His shoulders tensed as he reached the high-rise building. He loved Grant like a brother, but right now he didn't need to be reminded that the only woman he'd ever truly wanted was still out of reach. Still not his. And she had no clue how he felt about her.

"Nah. I'll call the security team, tell them to buzz you up. You've just gotta ask her out."

"I have." Countless times. They went out all the time. As friends.

When he'd first met Emerson she'd been coming off a bad breakup and definitely hadn't been interested in him. He'd known she was the one, so he hadn't pushed. The truth was, he'd never had a problem with women. They seemed to flock to him. Ever since he was fifteen. When he was a teenager, he'd reveled in it. Then he'd grown the hell up and gotten more discerning. Especially after spending years in war zones. He wasn't a teenager and he didn't want an easy lay.

He wanted Emerson. Forever. So he was playing things right. Unfortunately, around her he turned into a moron. He was suddenly that awkward teenager he'd never been during his actual teen years. It was like karma was punishing his ass for having it so easy with women for so many years.

"You're not trying hard enough... Hold on." There was a faint rustling in the background, then Grant talking to someone, then he was back on the line. "I just called it in. You're good to go."

"Thanks, man." Once they disconnected, he slipped his Bluetooth out of his ear and slid it into his jacket pocket.

Since he'd just gotten off shift at the police station, he was still in his suit. But his detective's badge was out of sight. His shoes made slight thudding sounds against the lobby floor as he strode across it. Once he reached the main security desk, he nodded at the security man he'd interacted with on many occasions—always when he was coming to see Emerson.

He set the bag of food on the counter. "I've got my service weapon on me." Even though the guy knew him he still wanted to inform him about his weapon.

The man nodded. "Figured you did. Grant said it's okay for you to take it up. How long you plan on being here?"

"Couple hours, maybe." Monday nights Emerson seemed to work late and this had become a standing ritual between them. He hadn't called her today though, had been so caught up with closing a case. But once he'd finished all the paperwork, he'd headed over here.

The need to see her, to be around her, was a live thing inside him. She was it for him and he'd known it pretty much from the moment they'd met. Man, she'd blindsided him too. He'd met her at one of Grant's get-togethers six months ago, and when his former partner had introduced her as "the new girl," he'd been a goner.

Her looks played into it a little, but after getting to know her that night, he hadn't been able to get her out of his head. She was smart, and a blend of sweet and sarcastic. He just liked being around her, plain and simple. Unfortunately, she hadn't seemed as interested. They'd gotten along great, but he knew when women were coming on to him and she never had.

Not once.

No coy looks or subtle flirtations. Nothing. They were just friends. Maybe he was a masochist, because that just seemed to make him want her more.

The elevator ride to her floor was quick as usual. And her floor was empty, again as usual, considering the time he was getting here. The security at Red Stone was tight, however, so the most protective part of him didn't mind how late she worked. Not that she'd asked him, and not like he had the right to an opinion. He also liked that she was working and not out with some douchebag.

He cared about her safety. Some intrinsic part of him simply needed to know she was cared for.

The hallway leading to her office was lined with prints of classic paintings, like most of the building. Everything here was designed to be soothing. Unlike where he worked. The PD was loud no matter the time of day or night, and the color of paint on the walls or type of art wouldn't make a damn difference.

When he reached her office, the door was slightly ajar. He pushed it open to find her in front of her computer screen, the soft glow highlighting her sharp cheekbones. Her long blonde hair was pulled up in a ponytail and her heels were lying haphazardly near the full-length window overlooking downtown.

He watched her for a long moment, taking in the myriad of facial expressions as she clicked away on the keyboard. He was certain she had no idea he was even there. When she got in the zone of working, everything else faded away. She made these adorable little sounds of frustration, then one of triumph before she nodded at the screen victoriously.

God, he adored her.

"You need better awareness," he murmured, stepping into the room.

She let out a squeak and glanced up at him, pinning him with those dark espresso eyes that completely captivated him. "You've got to stop sneaking up on me."

Frowning, she looked at her screen and her eyes widened. "Jeez, I didn't realize how late it was."

"I figured," he said dryly, setting the takeout bag on the front of her desk. He'd brought her favorite.

"You're my hero." She smiled, eyeing the big brown bag.

Yeah, he'd love to actually be her hero. Her lover, her…something other than her friend.

"Please tell me that's what I think it is."

He just snorted and started pulling out the utensils and paper plates. Of course it was. She loved a Chinese restaurant a few blocks away, called it a hidden gem in the city. She wasn't wrong. "Have I ever disappointed you?"

"No. I wasn't sure if you were coming today though, when you didn't call."

He flicked a glance at her at the tone in her voice. He couldn't quite pin it down, but something was off. "You can always call me too, you know."

"Yeah I know, but with that case you're working on, I didn't want to bother you. Figured you had a lot going on this week."

He'd never be too busy that he couldn't make time to talk to her. "I've wrapped everything up, for the most part." And thank God for that. Holidays seemed to bring out the crazy in people though—and crime never took a break—so he knew he'd be assigned another case probably tomorrow. Maybe sooner if a call came in tonight.

She turned off her computer screen, dimming it to black. Some of the things she worked on were confidential. Not just anyone could waltz up into the offices on her floor. The only reason he was able to was because of his relationship with Grant and the entire Caldwell family.

"I bet you skipped some paperwork though." Her half-smile was knowing as she rounded the desk, pulling her chair with her so they could eat on the same side. She was wearing a sweater dress that pulled at the soft swell of her breasts. The dress was definitely professional but it didn't hide anything. Her smooth, toned legs drew his eyes as they always did. Without her heels on she was about five feet five inches and he loved seeing her so relaxed around him—loved looking at her curves. Who was he kidding? He loved looking at all of her.

He lifted a shoulder as he pulled out a box of sesame chicken and broccoli. He slid it over to her, loving the way her eyes lit up as she eyed it.

"I seriously love you," she said, laughing. "I only had a protein bar today because of Lizzy. That woman is crazy."

His heart skipped a beat at the casual way she said the "L" word. He knew she didn't mean anything by it, and that was a huge disappointment. Jesus, what was wrong with him? He rolled his shoulders once and pulled out his Mongolian beef and rice.

"Why did she make you skip lunch?" Because a protein bar did not count as food.

Emerson shook her head, still laughing. "She's on this crazy exercise kick where she works out for her entire lunch break, running up and down all the flights of stairs in the entire building. More than once. She decided she needed a buddy and I'm apparently a sucker."

Carlito let out a short laugh and sat in the chair in front of her desk. "How long do you think you'll keep it up?" He knew she preferred yoga or Pilates to running and other cardio.

"Maybe another day or two. I'm working on a new job and know I'll be busy for the next couple weeks so I figured it was good to stretch my legs while I can."

For some reason those benign words made him think of stretching her legs out in a very different scenario. Stretching them around his waist or draping them over his shoulders as he buried his face between her legs. Clearing his throat, he shifted uncomfortably and focused on his food. "So…you headed to see your dad tonight?"

"Yeah." Her voice took on that odd tone again but when he looked at her, she was scooping out chicken onto her plate. "What are you up to after this?" Something about her voice was strained. It was slight, but he knew her well enough by now to pick up on it.

"I…thought I'd go with you." He always went with her to visit her dad in his assisted living facility. Which was more like a posh golf resort. Frowning, he set his fork down. "Unless you'd rather go alone?"

"No, I… I just talked to Camilla earlier and she made it sound like you couldn't go tonight."

"She did?" His oldest sister and Emerson talked all the time. They had ever since his sisters and mom had met Emerson at a Halloween party a month and a half ago.

"Yeah." Again with that weird tone. And he noticed she wouldn't look at him, was way too focused on her food.

"Well, she's wrong. I probably should have stayed late and finished up with that paperwork, but it'll wait until morning. I wouldn't miss seeing your old man." He loved the guy—Emerson Sr.—loved talking to him about his days in the Corps and hearing stories about Emerson when she was a kid. He liked being part of her life, knowing the people most important to her.

Her shoulders eased at that. "Well, good. He loves seeing you."

"What about you?" he asked.

"What about me?"

"Do you love seeing me?" he asked in a teasing tone—even if he did want to know the answer.

She rolled her eyes before giving him one of those heart-stopping grins that made him forget how to function, let alone speak. "You just brought me food. Of course I do."

One day he was going to put that smile on her face because he'd given her the best damn orgasm of her life. Because he loved her more than any other man ever would. He was going to convince her that they were meant to be together.

She was already one of the closest friends he'd ever had, and that was saying something. His family loved her, and hell, even if they didn't, he wouldn't care. He just needed to get his shit together. Christmas was soon and he planned to let her know how he felt then. Planned to give her a present that made it crystal clear how much she meant to him. If she didn't return his feelings...

He'd deal with it.

CHAPTER SEVEN

As Isa steered into her garage she frowned at the sight of headlights in her rearview mirror, pulling into her driveway. They quickly went off, making her frown deepen.

She lived in a quiet neighborhood. She'd rented for about a month when she moved to Miami, but then she'd found this adorable little ranch-style home in a quiet cul-de-sac neighborhood that she loved. It was filled with palm trees and pools in practically every backyard, and she loved everything about it, including her neighbors. Everyone here knew everyone and they looked out for each other.

She pulled out her pepper spray from her purse and quickly exited the vehicle. It wasn't too late for visitors, but no one ever stopped by for a random visit and she didn't recognize the vehicle.

When she saw Graysen's familiar form step out of an SUV, that momentary spike of panic left her body. Maybe there had been an emergency at work?

She tossed the pepper spray onto the driver's seat and hurried out of her garage. "Hey, what's going on?" she asked, her heels clicking on the pavement.

Instead of answering, he opened the door behind the driver's side and a bundle of gray and white fur jumped out. Yipping excitedly, Peaches raced toward her and as she jumped into the air, Isa caught the adorable mutt in her arms. She was inundated with licks and kisses as she buried her face against Peaches' head.

"What are you doing here?" she asked Graysen.

He wore the same suit he'd had on today, sans tie. The top button of his dress shirt was undone and for some insane reason she wished she'd been the one to take off that tie, to unbutton his shirt, to...

Nope, nope, nope. Not going there.

He lifted a shoulder. "Peaches missed you."

"There's no emergency at work?"

He shrugged again, all casual nonchalance. "Not that I know of."

Her eyes widened. "So you just decided to stop by with your dog? Out of the blue?" *Like we're freaking friends?*

"Yep."

She narrowed her gaze at him, tried to keep her annoyance clear, but it was hard to look serious and frustrated when Peaches was licking her face, just begging for attention. "How'd you even know where I liv— Never mind. Don't answer that." He'd probably found out long before he started working for Red Stone.

"Aren't you going to invite us in?"

"I must be out of my mind, but come on." She didn't want to stand outside and have whatever conversation he wanted to have while any of her neighbors might see and come out to check on her. She turned back toward the garage, and, still holding Peaches, grabbed her purse and laptop bag from her car before shutting the door. Once inside her mudroom she disarmed her alarm system, but only after making sure Graysen turned around. Not that it would likely matter. He would probably have no issue breaking into her place if he truly wanted to.

Before they'd taken two steps into her kitchen, Graysen stepped in front of her, his weapon drawn. A little burst of panic set in before she realized what he was doing.

The man was a total freak sometimes. Even when she'd thought of him as Michael, he'd been the same: vigilant about security.

"Sure, go ahead and sweep my house as if you have every right," she muttered more to herself than him as he made his way through the kitchen to one of the attached rooms.

He clearly wasn't listening and didn't care anyway.

"You are in luck," she murmured against Peaches, who'd stopped squirming and was now sitting contently in Isa's arms. "I've got a treat for you."

Peaches knew what the word treat was and started wiggling again, licking Isa's face as if she loved her more than anyone in the world. Unexpected tears stung her eyes. She'd really missed this sweet dog. She'd even contemplated getting one of her own when she moved to Miami, but she'd been a mess a year ago and hadn't been ready.

Now... Yeah, she could get one now. Of course, no dog compared to Peaches.

Reaching into her pantry, she held onto the dog with one arm and opened the plastic bag of fake bacon treats. "One or two, do you think?" she asked.

Peaches let out two little yips, as if she actually understood.

Laughing, Isa gave her the two strips and when she wiggled to be freed, set her down. Peaches scurried away, probably to hide one of the strips, right as Graysen walked back into the kitchen. He was sheathing his weapon as Peaches raced by him.

"So any dangers lurking in my secured house?" He clearly knew the security system had been armed.

"You're good." He frowned slightly at the bag of treats. "Why do you have dog treats?"

"Babysat a neighbor's dog not too long ago."

"Ah."

"So…why the heck are you here?"

"I wanted to see you." Heat flared in his blue eyes as he watched her.

She didn't like that she was affected by that look—and his mere presence. "That's not an answer."

"It's the truth. I told you that if in one week you're done with me, I'll walk away from the job. We have six days left."

"That doesn't give you the right to just show up at my house unannounced." But it was so typical Graysen. He could be incredibly pushy when he wanted. Which…she'd liked about him. *Before.* Back then she'd liked *everything* about him.

Before she'd discovered what a liar he was. Before her father had died.

"I know."

"But you did it anyway?"

He leaned against the island in her kitchen, looking at ease here, as if he belonged. Or more likely that was just wishful thinking on her part. "Two people after Gina infiltrated your computer today. I wanted to make sure you were safe." He said it as if he truly had been concerned about her. Which, okay, wasn't actually a surprise.

"No one there knows who I really am." She always took precautions when she worked on a Miami job. When she was out of town it was easier to maintain anonymity, but when she was in her own city she had to be careful for sensitive jobs. And the one they were on was definitely sensitive. People were afraid they might be losing their jobs because of her. Not only that, someone was stealing from the aeronautical company. Clearly some employees were going to be let go because three employees, including Gina Scott, had copied information from her laptop.

Isa still couldn't believe the three of them thought she'd be stupid enough to just leave her laptop lying around unlocked. But given enough time and what they thought had been an opportunity, three individuals had sneaked into her office in the middle of the day. The only miracle was that they hadn't run into each other while doing it. The video footage Graysen had gotten was pretty damning too.

"And I don't think I was followed home." Well, except by Graysen, but he might have just come to her house since he would have had her address. The man was too skilled at getting information to not know where she lived.

"You weren't followed. Except by me." He sounded positive about that, and if anyone would know, it would be him. She might not know what most of his training had entailed, but he'd worked for the CIA for eight years—and been in the Marine Corps before that. He'd certainly fooled her.

She stared at him for a long moment and tried to bury all the emotions that wanted to push their way to the surface. Emotions she should have buried long ago. He simply watched her right back with those bright blue eyes she could easily drown in. She'd gotten caught up in his gaze more than once in the past. It was like he ensnared her, and once she was hooked he was impossible to escape from.

Right now she had no idea what he was thinking. He had that neutral expression in place. The neutrality did nothing to hide the savage edge to the man. There were handsome men and then there were men like Graysen, who fell into their own category. He was good-looking, all right, and knew it. But there was an intangible edge to him that rolled off him in waves, warning he was trained and lethal. And…she liked that about him.

She cleared her throat, feeling unnerved by her physical reaction to him. "You don't have to make sure I get home safely every night." Because the thought of him coming into her home for the next week was too much to deal with. He was too much to deal with.

"You're my priority." His voice was low and somehow sensual.

"This job is the priority."

"Not to me." He rounded the island, closing the distance so only about four feet stood between them. Definitely not enough space.

Being this close to him had her entire body heating up and her nipples tightening. *Stupid physical reaction!* It was hard to remember to breathe when he was this close. All day she'd managed to maintain a certain distance from Graysen. Even when they'd been watching the video feeds together, she'd been so focused on work that it had been easier to tune out his presence. Obviously not completely, because he was Graysen. But still, easier.

Having him in her personal space, her domain, was jarring and messing with her head. And after what he'd just said? Yep, no response for that.

He took a step closer. "You want to have dinner together?"

Against her will, her gaze briefly strayed to his mouth. She mentally shook herself. "Not tonight."

He took another step, his advances slow and precise. A patient panther, stalking its prey. "But another night?"

She cleared her throat again, willing her voice to work. "What do you think you're doing?" She hated that her voice trembled, hated that he had a sort of power over her.

"I've got a week, Isa. I want to spend time with you when we're not at work. I've missed you, thought about you every damn day." The sincerity in his eyes pierced her. He lifted a hand as if he wanted to touch her, but quickly dropped it.

Yeah, well, she wanted a lot of things, mainly to rewrite the past so they didn't have such a shitty history. And she didn't want to be affected by him. Not only that, she'd never agreed to see him after work hours. "Call or text me, then. Don't just show up at my house." If he did that, she could just blow him off.

He opened his mouth but her cell phone buzzed in her purse, the sound music to her ears. Turning away from him, she grabbed it, glad to see Emerson's name on the screen.

"Hey," she said, answering on the second ring.

"Hey yourself. I'm heading out for the day but just sent updated files to both you and Graysen on the three top suspects."

Isa wasn't surprised Emerson was just now leaving work. The woman always worked late. She also got to work from home sometimes and had leeway with her schedule—and got paid very, very well for her skills. "Thanks for letting me know."

"They've all got interesting financials, but take a good look at Gina Scott."

"Will do."

"I'll be in later tomorrow, probably around ten, but I'll have my phone on me if you need me."

"Okay. Tell your dad hi for me."

She could practically hear Emerson smiling through the phone. "I will. He said thanks for the popcorn tin and wants to know when to expect more."

Isa smiled, glad he'd enjoyed it. "I'll get more in time for Christmas."

They talked a minute longer and when they disconnected she felt more like herself, more in control. Setting the phone on the countertop, she turned to find Graysen leaning against the island, looking all casual and sexy as he watched her.

"Emerson sent us updated info. And...I need you to go, Graysen." She needed space from him. Having him sprung on her for this job wasn't as easy to handle as she'd thought it would be. Yes, she could be professional. "We need boundaries. Showing up here? I'm not okay with that."

His jaw tightened once but he nodded. "Okay. I'm sorry."

She blinked, surprised he'd acquiesced so easily.

"Have dinner with me this week?" he continued. "We can meet somewhere." The slight edge of desperation in his voice took her off guard, almost made her say yes.

But... "I just want to get through this job."

He nodded once, let out a short whistle then Peaches raced back into the kitchen, her nails clicking on the tile. Instead of running to Graysen, she charged Isa again.

Heart melting, Isa picked her up, snuggled her against her chest.

"I'm not giving up on us." His quiet words had the effect of a grenade going off.

There is no us she wanted to shout at him, but the words stuck in her throat. Somewhere, deep down, though she didn't want to acknowledge it, she knew they could have something incredible together.

But she was terrified of all the ugly baggage between them. Worried that she'd never be able to move past his betrayal and would just resent him if she let him back into her life again. If she did that and things spiraled downward...

She just didn't know if it was worth the almost guaranteed heartache. She wasn't a masochist.

She glanced away from him, used Peaches as an excuse for a distraction and grabbed another treat for her. "I'll walk you to your SUV," was all she managed to get out.

Because telling him anything else wasn't an option.

CHAPTER EIGHT

Stepping into her dad's office, Isa leaned against the doorframe as her dad spoke into his phone. Even on a Sunday afternoon he was working; no surprise. Larger than life, her dad smiled at her and held up a finger that she should wait before he continued his conversation.

Isa had to get up early for a meeting tomorrow and her place was in DC. Sometimes she stayed over at her dad's but his estate was in Virginia and while the drive wasn't terrible, her boyfriend Michael had asked her to stay at his place overnight. Had said he wanted to talk to her about something. Whatever that something was had butterflies dancing in her stomach. She was actually running late, but she'd call him as soon as she was on the road.

"You leaving, baby girl?" Her dad's booming voice cut through her train of thought. Everything about him was loud, larger than life.

Shaking herself, she nodded and stepped farther into the room. "Yeah. I've got some work to do before my meeting tomorrow." And okay, she wanted to get plenty of naked time with Michael. Not like she'd be saying that out loud, however.

"Thanks for coming over for lunch," he said, standing and rounding his desk. "I don't see you enough lately."

"I know." They'd always had weekly lunches or dinners, either in the city or at his house. Usually in the city, since he worked for a big defense contractor. "I'm hoping after Christmas things will slow down." Usually January and February were her slowest months, and from what she knew, her dad didn't have a big contract coming up.

"Well, I've got to head out the day after Christmas. Probably going to sign a new contract soon. Which will mean travel." He winced slightly, looking guilty.

Disappointment filled her but she hid it. "It's okay. I always understand work." And she did. Her mom had died in childbirth, so it had just been the two of them from the beginning. She knew he dated, but he'd never brought anyone home. And he'd worked incredibly hard to send her to the best schools. He'd given her everything she'd ever wanted or needed. When she was younger she hadn't appreciated how much he'd done—what kid did?—but now she understood how much he'd sacrificed for her and how many opportunities she'd been given.

"I know that you do." He looped his arms around her, pulling her into a bear hug before he kissed the top of her head. "Text me when you're home. I want to know you made it safe."

"I will." She was almost thirty but it didn't matter to her dad. She'd always be his baby girl. And she was okay with that.

"So is that man of yours planning on proposing any time soon?" he asked, stepping back and eyeing her.

"Ah, I think it's too soon." Though if Michael asked she would say yes. Which seemed insane to admit, even to herself. The chemistry she had with him was unlike anything she'd ever experienced before, and when they were together Michael had eyes for no one but her. She felt treasured and safe in a way she'd never expected or thought possible. None of her previous boyfriends held a candle to Michael. He could be a little *overprotective and worried about her safety, but there were a lot worse qualities she could have in a significant other.*

"Four months isn't too soon. I knew your mom was the one after a month." *His dark eyebrows pulled together, his brow furrowing.*

Shaking her head, she just gave her dad another hug. She'd heard the story a million times, it felt like. Her mom had been waiting tables at a diner and he'd been one of her customers. He'd been smitten from the start, but it had taken a week to convince her mom to go out with him. "I've really got to run, but I promise to let you know when I'm home." *She'd told Michael she'd leave a while ago, had even packed up her car—including her cell phone. He'd probably called her, wanting to know where she was.*

Stepping out into the hallway, she started to head for the front door but caught herself at the stairwell and headed back up it instead. She made her way to one of the guest rooms where she'd left her laptop. As she picked it up, something caught her eye. She glanced out one of the windows onto her father's huge estate and frowned. The two buttercream curtains were pulled back, revealing acres and acres of rolling green grassland. The front of the property was covered in trees, mainly live oaks. But she'd thought she'd seen a flash of black dart behind one of the trees.

Laptop tucked under her arm, she moved closer to the window, the warmth of the afternoon sun bathing her face as she peered outside. More of the yard and the long, winding driveway that looped out to the west side of the property came into view.

Her breath caught in her throat as she tried to digest what she was seeing.

A line of dark SUVs were rolling down the drive, some with flashing blue lights, and a swarm of men dressed in all black were rushing the house.

Ohmygodohmygodohmygod!

She was racing for the door, ready to shout for her dad, when an explosion sounded downstairs.

"Dad!" she screamed as she spilled out into the hallway. Fear lanced through her, sharp and stinging. What the hell was going on?

At the top of the stairs she saw that the explosion had been someone ramming the front door open. It hung off its hinges and two men in tactical gear with huge freaking guns pointed them up the stairs at her.

"Hands in the air, now!" one of them shouted.

Without thought she dropped the laptop and threw her hands up. Her heart was an erratic, out-of-control beat in her chest as her computer tumbled down the stairs, clacking along the wooden steps.

"Face down on the ground!" the same man shouted.

Even as she was complying, falling to her knees at the top of the stairs, both men were racing up toward her. Seconds later one of them yanked her arms behind her back and slapped handcuffs on her.

"Dad!" she screamed for her father even as the armed man yanked her to her feet. She could see the FBI logo on their vests so she knew they were from the government, but none of this made sense. Why would they be raiding her father's house when he worked for a defense contractor? He was one of the good guys.

Pop. Pop.

She jumped at the sound of gunfire. Two more sharp pops went off in quick succession. Then glass shattered.

Oh God, her father. Was he injured? Before she could do or say anything...

Crack. Crack. Crack. Crack. Crack.

The sound of staccato gunfire made her flinch even as the armed man spoke to her. She had no idea what he was saying, couldn't comprehend the words. No, she could only focus on the terrifying sounds of gunfire in her childhood home and the people swarming in through the broken front door. They were like roaches, all dressed in black.

"Where's my father? Is he okay?" *she shouted, unable to get her voice or her heartbeat under control as the man led her downstairs. She was vaguely aware of the other man having left them and storming into the guest room she'd just been in. Maybe they were looking for more people? Maybe they thought someone else was here?*

She struggled to push the fear aside. This had to be a mistake. Whatever was going on they would fix it. But she just needed to find her father, needed to see that he was okay.

The man leading her downstairs didn't respond, just spoke into an earpiece. She wanted to keep shouting at him, to keep screaming, but knew it wouldn't do any good.

As they reached the bottom of the stairs Michael stormed through the front door. She froze, looking at him, not comprehending why her boyfriend was here. There were so many people hustling in and out of her father's home.

She felt as if she was watching this happen to someone else, that this was some nightmare she'd wake up from.

"Get those cuffs off her!" *Michael shouted at the man next to her.*

Fear for him slid through her veins like slow-moving ice, sharp and burning. She started to tell him to back off or something, worried that this armed man would handcuff him too, but to her surprise she felt the handcuffs being released. The armed man practically shoved her at Michael before hurrying off upstairs, his boots stomping loudly on the treads.

Blinking, she stared up at Michael, trying to find her voice and trying to understand this entire situation. "What are you—"

That was when she realized he was wearing a jacket that had the FBI logo on it. A blue windbreaker that seemed too light for the current weather, not that it mattered one bit.

She blinked again, frozen in place. "You're FBI?" she asked stupidly. He'd told her that he was a security contractor for a private company. Just like her father.

His jaw tightened. "Come on. I need you out of here." He wrapped his fingers around her upper arm.

She pulled back from him, ignoring the strangers moving around them as if they had every right to be here. "My father—"

He didn't let her go even though she tried to yank away. His grip only tightened. "I need you out of here now!"

"I need to see my father!" Her voice rose with every word. Her entire body trembled and all she knew was that she'd heard gunfire.

In her childhood home.

And her father wasn't calling for her.

A sick sensation pervaded her, making her stomach lurch. "My father?" she whispered.

Even though she was certain Michael didn't hear her over the cacophony of noise, he shook his head, his jaw tight and his expression tormented. He turned slightly to the side and she saw an earpiece.

His grip dropped for an instant as one of those armed men stepped up to him, spoke in quiet tones. It was the only opening she needed. Shoving away from him, she sprinted down the hallway. Two steel bands encircled her from behind as she reached the doorway of her dad's office.

But it was too late.

Her father was sprawled on his blue and green Persian rug, the crimson of his blood staining it and him. A gun lay near one of his limp hands. Blood covered the front of what had been a pale cornflower blue shirt, one she'd given him for his last birthday. Two huge holes gaped in his chest and there was a bright red stain in the middle of his forehead.

Oh... God. No, no, no.

"Noooooo!" She realized she was screaming only as Michael lifted her into his arms and tossed her over his shoulder, racing her away from her worst nightmare.

Isa's eyes opened with a start, her heart racing out of control, sweat dotting her upper lip and dripping down her back despite the cool temperature in her bedroom. She hadn't had that particular nightmare—which wasn't a nightmare, but a memory—in months.

Trembling slightly, she slid out of bed and headed to the bathroom. After splashing cold water on her face she stepped into her bedroom and realized it was only ten o'clock. She'd crashed an hour ago, abnormally early for her to go to bed, but she'd just wanted to shut out the real world, and sleep had been the best way to do that.

Picking her phone up off the nightstand, she texted Mara. *You awake?*

Less than ten seconds later her phone rang. When Isa saw Mara's number on the screen, she smiled. "Hey, you didn't have to call."

"I know, but it's late for you to be texting. What's up?"

"I..." Ugh, she felt like an idiot. Why had she texted? She didn't want to say she'd had a bad dream. It made her sound like a five-year-old. Her throat tightened as unexpected tears stung her eyes. Some days she'd be totally fine about everything—or at least able to cope—and then she'd have a nightmare and it was like she was drowning in memories and grief all over again.

"You want some company?" Mara asked softly.

Isa blinked, the question taking her by surprise. "Oh, no, it's too late. I just texted because..." She let out a short laugh. "Because working with Graysen is harder than I imagined. But this can wait until tomorrow."

"Harrison had to go out of town tonight. A quick trip up to Orlando to meet with a potential client."

"Oh, right." She'd actually known that, had talked to him earlier about what they'd discovered so far at Raptor Aeronautical.

"So, I'm alone anyway and I can't sleep without Harrison. I'll be over in a bit with a bottle of wine. Pick out a movie for us. None of those stupid romantic comedies." She hung up before Isa could respond, as was Mara's way.

A very small part of Isa felt bad, wanted to call Mara back and tell her not to come over simply because Isa was feeling emotional and out of sorts.

After losing pretty much her entire social circle after her father's treachery had been splashed all over the news a year ago, she'd been so damn alone when she'd moved to Miami. No one from DC or even her college friends would return her calls. She'd become a leper overnight.

Landing the job with Red Stone Security had been unexpected and a gift in more ways than one. From that first day, Mara had taken her under her wing and made her feel accepted.

Even though it made her feel a little pathetic that her friend was coming over so late because she was feeling weak and needy, she didn't care. Right now she needed a friend.

CHAPTER NINE

Graysen steered into the parking garage of his high-rise condo. He'd stayed at Isa's house, watching as the lights went off one by one. But then he'd started to feel like a stalker so he'd forced himself to leave. Going to her home had been a risk, a stupid one. And the reason he'd given her for showing up—that he'd been worried about her safety—had been equally stupid. She wasn't in danger.

He'd just needed to see her. It had been selfish on his part, but where Isa was concerned he didn't seem to think clearly.

As he got out of his SUV, memories of the day her father died assaulted him. Isa should have been in DC, far away from everything that went down on that fateful day. But because of bullshit timing, she'd seen everything and her life had been ripped apart. His too, because he'd screwed up everything with her that day.

Not that it mattered. The only thing he cared about was her. She'd ripped his world apart simply by being in it. If he could go back in time... *Hell.* He didn't know what he'd do. Her father had been selling state secrets, had betrayed his country to the highest bidder on more than one occasion.

But Isa had been innocent in it all. Not that it had mattered once the media ripped her father's life apart.

Hers had been destroyed right along with it. She'd lost her job, her friends, everything. Guilt raked through him at the knowledge that he'd been part of that.

It was why she'd moved to Miami, to escape the bitter scrutiny and judgment. She'd have never been able to get a decent job in DC again anyway. Not after what had happened. She'd always be looked at with suspicion no matter how innocent she was. There'd been another scandal a week after the story of her father's treachery and death broke, something to do with multiple senators being caught up in a prostitution ring. It was the only thing that had allowed her to start over as easily as she had without further media scrutiny. People cared more about sex, and the politicians' story had been salacious.

Instead of walking to the elevator, he took Peaches out of the garage and headed around the big building to the area designated for pets. A bright full moon illuminated the grassy area. As Peaches took care of her business, that gut-wrenching afternoon replayed in his mind.

Maybe because it was close to Christmas, or maybe because he'd spent most of the day with Isa, but that day was all he could think about.

His heart raced a little faster as the phone rang, as he waited for Isa to pick up. He'd just gotten a call from his boss that today they would be infiltrating her father's estate and arresting him. The man had just taken the bait they'd laid out for him, agreeing to meet with a new buyer to potentially sell the identities of five covert agents. As a defense contractor he wouldn't normally have access to that kind of information but they'd discovered he'd been working with multiple hackers and using his access to areas of high-level security in different government buildings to help get those hackers infiltrated into private intranet networks.

"Hey, babe." Isa's voice was light, her tone easy.

He forced his voice to remain steady when all he wanted to do was tell her the truth. But he couldn't. "Hey, are you headed back to the city yet?"

"Soon, I promise. Just spending time with my dad."

He needed to get a time frame from her but didn't want to tip her off that it mattered what time she got back home. The FBI had moved up their infiltration day and time. Isa wasn't supposed to be anywhere near the estate when this happened. That had been one of his main concerns. Shit like this happened all the time, something he understood. But it had never been personal like this before. He'd never expected someone like her—and had never slept with anyone involved in a case before either. She was so sweet, open, and giving. She made a lot of money analyzing work effectiveness for various companies but gave so much back to the community with her free time. It was hard to believe she was her father's daughter, now that he knew how treacherous the man really was.

"Well hurry back. I miss you. And I have something I want to talk to you about." He hated himself even as he said the words. He needed to tell her everything they'd discovered about her father. He wanted to do it in a calm setting where it was just the two of them. Not that it would matter where he told her—the news that her father was a traitor to his country would devastate her. But he still wanted to break the news to her as easy as he could.

"Are you breaking up with me?" she asked jokingly, clearly knowing that he never wanted to do that.

When he was with her he might pretend to be Michael, but he was still able to be himself, to be Graysen. And he hated himself more and more every day for lying to her face. But too many men and women had died because of the information her father had leaked. People who mattered to him. He had a duty to his country and to all the other people out there who could become a target, could be tortured, murdered and worse because their identities were sold to the highest bidder.

"No." But you'll probably never want to see me again.

"Okay, then I won't push you to tell me what it is. I'll be leaving in the next couple minutes."

"You know I love you, right?" The words stuck in his throat even though they were true. Soon she would look at him in a new light, would see him for the liar he was. He just prayed that she could forgive him because a world without Isa in it was not a world he wanted to live in. And if she ended things with him... Hell, he couldn't go there. He just needed to get through this day.

"I love you too..." There was a rustling, then her voice was muffled for a moment. "Hey, I've got to run, but I'll see you soon."

He glanced at his phone even though he already knew the time. If she left soon, she would be away from the estate when everything went down. That was the only thing that made him feel nominally better about this whole screwed up situation.

Graysen scrubbed a hand over his face and tried to mentally shake off the memory, but it was useless. "Come on, girl." He patted his leg and Peaches ran up to him, the most loyal dog. He'd never admitted it to anyone, but if it wasn't for Peaches, the last year would have been even harder.

At least when he came home at night there was someone there happy to see him. Unfortunately, it wasn't Isa. But he wasn't giving up on her, on them. He simply couldn't.

Part of him wanted to give her the file he'd been sitting on. The file that had all the dark truth about her father—what he'd done, how many people he'd gotten killed and in some cases, tortured. But…he didn't want to be the cause of more of Isa's pain. It would go a long way in explaining why Graysen had done what he'd done, but he didn't know that he wanted to be the one to give her all that brutal truth.

* * *

Emerson wrapped her arms around herself as she and Carlito stepped outside into the chilly night air. She loved that he came to her father's nursing home with her every week. Everyone loved her dad, and some of her other friends came with her as well when they could, but those were her girlfriends.

Carlito was… Well, she wasn't quite sure what he was. They were friends, had been for the last six months. Lately, however, she was starting to have feelings for him. And definitely not the "friends only" kind.

She nearly jumped when he placed his jacket around her shoulders. He was a lot broader and wider than her. He had a lean, cut physique, something she didn't want to be noticing. They were friends—she shouldn't be so sexually aware of the man.

When they first met she'd been aware of how attractive he was. Obviously—she'd have to be blind not to realize how sexy the man was. He was handsome and polished, not what she pictured when she thought of a detective.

But he was always put together, his suits perfect and pressed. She could never keep herself so impeccable, but it seemed effortless for him. His bronzed skin seemed to glow year-round and his cheekbones would make supermodels envious. There was an edge to him, however. Probably to do with his job, considering how much death and other awful things he saw. So when he looked at her with those piercing gray eyes it was hard to ignore the sex appeal factor.

So yeah, she'd noticed all of that when they'd first met, but she hadn't been thinking about the opposite sex in terms of dating or anything romantic at the time. Not after her last breakup.

"Thanks," she said, pulling the jacket tighter around her. It was way too big and smelled like him, a distinctive spicy cologne that made her want to inhale deeply.

She'd left her thick coat in the car, thinking she wouldn't need it. But it felt as if it had dropped ten degrees since they'd been inside. Or more likely the heat had been turned up so much in there that it just felt colder now. The fact that he was so considerate touched her. Her father had commented on it, because he seemed to think Carlito wanted more than friendship. He always asked her when she and Carlito were going to get married. She nearly snorted at the thought. This sexy detective wasn't going to be settling down anytime soon. She knew what kind of reputation he had.

"So are you still coming over for Christmas?" he asked.

"Of course, unless... Did your plans change or something?" Carlito's sister Camilla had said something to Emerson earlier today about him dating someone new, so she wasn't sure if that was why he was asking. Six months ago the thought of him dating wouldn't have fazed her, but now...

She didn't like that ugly, twisting sensation in the pit of her stomach. It wasn't like he belonged to her. It wasn't like they were anything other than friends. But she found herself feeling oddly possessive of him lately. Okay, maybe more than just lately. It had been a gradual buildup until one day she realized—she wanted more than friendship from Carlito. Way more.

It was part of the reason she hadn't called him earlier today. When Camilla had told her he was seeing someone else she hadn't wanted to hear the truth from him. Emerson wasn't sure she'd be able to act nonchalant about it. She wondered why he hadn't said anything— even as she was happy that he *hadn't*. She didn't want to hear about him and some other woman.

He let out a short laugh. "Never. My mom would kill me if I didn't show up for Christmas. And she'd probably kill me if I didn't bring you."

The sharpest sense of relief slid through her veins. She adored his whole family but especially his mother. Her own mom had died when she'd been young and part of her had always felt as if she was missing something. "You never told me what I should bring."

"Just yourself. And your dad, if you think he's up to it." He gave her a strange look as they reached her car.

They'd driven separately since they lived in opposite directions, and now she wished they'd ridden together in one vehicle because she wanted to spend more time with him. An hour or two at a time was never enough. It didn't matter that they talked on the phone—when they got to spend time together she always wanted more, more, *more*.

"What?" she asked, feeling self-conscious under his scrutiny.

"Is everything okay? You seemed a little distracted today." The concern in his gaze was real and she adored how sincere he was about everything—and not just with her, but with everyone. It was why he was such a good detective.

What she'd heard about him from others was different than the man she'd come to know. One of her coworkers had mentioned that she thought Carlito was a player, but so far Emerson hadn't seen any truth in that. Or he could just keep that stuff on the down-low. The thought of him with another woman, touching her, kissing her... *Nope.* Even thinking about it hurt too much.

"I'm good. Just have a lot going on with this new job." She wished she could tell him about it, but in addition to the standard nondisclosure she'd signed when she'd been hired by Red Stone Security, she'd also had to sign another nondisclosure specifically for this job.

"Okay." He nodded slightly, those pale gray eyes she could get lost in narrowing as if he didn't believe her.

Some days... *Gah.* Some days she swore she saw hints of heat in his gaze. But that was likely wishful thinking on her part.

"Do you have plans Saturday?" she blurted before she could stop herself. If he was dating someone new, of course he would already have plans.

To her relief, he shook his head. "Unless something comes up at work, then I'm free."

"One of my friends mentioned something about a boat parade. And I've never been so I wanted to know if you wanted to go with me? Since you're the local." She'd moved here from Orlando when she'd gotten the job with Red Stone, and while she'd been to Miami over the years she'd never been here for the holidays.

"I'd love to." He nodded, that delicious mouth of his curving up into a smile that made her think wicked, wicked things. Mainly naked fantasies about him—she'd seen him in swim trunks at one of the get-togethers at Grant and Belle's place, and holy hotness, the man looked incredible without a shirt on. He should go around half naked all the time.

And at the thought, her face heated up. She cursed her fair coloring in that moment and hoped he didn't notice.

Before she could respond he continued. "I'll pick you up at four on Saturday? That way we can be sure to get there early and get a good spot."

"Sounds perfect." If he was going with her, then he wasn't with some other woman. Maybe his sister had been wrong about him dating someone new. The truth was, if Emerson was seeing a man like Carlito, she'd want all his spare time. Who was she kidding? They weren't dating and she still wanted to see him all the time. She hated that she was too much of a coward to ask him if he was currently single.

But she definitely wasn't brave enough to make a move on him. After getting burned so badly before she still didn't quite trust her taste in men. And if she was really honest with herself, she was more scared of screwing up the friendship they had by asking if he wanted something more with her. She didn't want to risk ruining one of the best relationships she'd ever had with anyone.

With him, she was always herself. Never felt like she had to put on a show or be anything other than who she was. So the thought of losing that? Nope, she wasn't going to risk it.

But if he made a move on her? That was a different story.

CHAPTER TEN

Going about his daily business when he'd be leaving the country soon, leaving his entire life behind and never looking back, was harder than Alan had thought. Excitement and fear hummed through him 24/7.

It was impossible to sleep and he was barely eating. He just wanted to be done with this life, to have his money and get the hell out of this country with the woman he loved. No more ex-wife, no more debt. Nothing but sandy beaches where he'd live like a king. If he could just get through a couple more days without detection.

When a phone buzzed in his jacket pocket it took him a moment to realize it was the disposable phone he'd been using to contact his buyers and other individuals helping him to get out of the country once he had his money.

A quick glance at the screen revealed that it was a private caller—no surprise. Anyone who called this phone had a blocked line. He answered immediately. "Yes?"

"It's me."

He recognized Yuri's voice. The Russian contact who'd first reached out to him about a way for him to make a lot of money.

From the digging Alan had done into his buyers he knew that Yuri himself was an exceptional hacker.

So when Hamilton had brought in two new employees this week, he'd sent their information to Yuri to look into them. At this point, he couldn't take any more risks. Everything had to go off without a hitch.

"What have you found out about the two newest employees?" Because there was no other reason for Yuri to be calling right now—unless something had gone wrong with the current op. Ice slid through his veins at the thought. Everything was good on his end.

"The woman works for a company called Red Stone Security. Her name is Isa Harper, not Johnson. I'm still not certain what she does there, but she doesn't work for the company listed on the resume you sent me."

He felt all the blood drain from his face, his hands going clammy as he listened. He lived in Miami, knew exactly what Red Stone Security was. They were involved in private security for dignitaries and other wealthy individuals, but they had other divisions as well. Top secret ones.

Yuri continued. "The founder is a man named Keith Caldwell. Three sons now run the company full-time. They have ties with various government agencies and it appears as if the father used to work for the CIA."

That only confirmed the rumors he'd heard. He cleared his throat. "And you have no idea why she's here?"

"No, but it can't be good. And there is more. Her father's name was Jeffrey Harper."

Jeffrey Harper? The name sounded familiar—he racked his brain trying to think where he'd heard it before. But Yuri continued again before he could ask who the man was.

"He was killed a little over a year ago by your FBI. He was selling state secrets to the highest bidders all over the world." There was a short pause. "I did business with him once about five years ago. His information was solid."

"What does that mean?" The woman's father had been a traitor to his country? How did that tie in with anything going on here? Why would she be working here now?

"Maybe nothing. It's just information I have, and you wanted to know everything about her. I do not like her involvement with your company this close to the end of our operation."

Yeah, no shit. "I spoke to Hamilton, and she shouldn't be here longer than another week or so. It's possible that she really is here to help him clean house." Hamilton had made it clear Isa was working closely with him to see where they could make cuts. It made sense his boss wouldn't be honest about what company she worked for. Hamilton wouldn't want to give anyone information about her if she was basically targeting jobs.

"I still don't like it."

Neither did he. "What do you want me to do?"

"Keep an eye on her for now. Did you implant the software into her laptop to shadow her?"

"I did." He'd had someone else do it as a safety measure to himself. Someone Alan considered expendable.

"So far she's been looking into various employee files but there's been nothing to make it seem as if she's looking for..." He cleared his throat, not about to say the words out loud. His office and this phone might be secure, but some things he didn't need to spell out. "I've also started monitoring the phone in her office." Something Yuri already knew, but he wanted it clear he had this woman under surveillance.

That he was in complete control.

When Yuri just grunted, he continued. "What about the man, Garret Evans?"

"So far he appears to be who he says he is. His resume appears to be legitimate, and if it is, he has a lot of experience in your field. According to the paper trail I followed, he and your boss have been in contact for a while, farther back than when you decided to sell your...product."

He nearly snorted at the word "product." He wasn't selling a tangible item. Not technically. But product was as good a word as any.

"So it seems unlikely that he brought this Evans in because he's suspicious of you. More likely he's been trying to lure him away from his previous job for a while and Evans finally agreed. That is what it looks like on my end."

"Okay, good." At least one of the new hires was a non-issue. The woman, though...

He didn't like her snooping around all their files even if it was her job. From what he'd garnered, she had unlimited access to everything. That alone was terrifying.

When his intercom buzzed, he quickly ended the call with Yuri. "Yes?" he said after a moment.

"Something big is going on," his assistant Cynthia whispered from out in her office.

The excitement in her voice made him stand without answering. Opening the door, he headed into her office area. She had her cell phone pressed up against her ear and was whispering to someone. Seeing her on her cell phone surprised him since she was always the professional. And cell phones were banned at work, for the most part.

After whispering "Hold on" to whoever was on the other line, she covered the receiver of her phone. "I just heard from someone on the fifth floor that Gina Scott is getting arrested." Her blue eyes were wide, almost as if she was asking *him* for confirmation.

Shock reverberated through him. If Scott was being arrested, it was something he *should* be aware of. Instead of responding audibly, Alan just gave Cynthia a nod and headed toward the elevators. As he reached the closed doors his regular cell phone buzzed in his pocket. Because of his position in the company, he was one of the few people permitted to have his cell phone on him. Of course, no one knew about his burner phone.

He answered on the first ring when he saw that it was Hamilton. "Yes?"

"I need to see you in my office, *now*."

"Is this about Gina Scott getting arrested?" He couldn't believe the woman had been arrested, couldn't even imagine what for. She seemed like such a straight arrow. She was bitchy enough, always had a stick up her ass about something. But she'd been good at her job. Or so he'd thought.

"Yes." Hamilton disconnected before he could ask anything else.

That wasn't out of the ordinary for Hamilton, otherwise Alan might be panicking more. Taking a deep breath, he stepped inside the elevator and pressed the button for the floor above him. If Hamilton knew what he was up to, he was totally and utterly screwed. But it was too late to run now.

CHAPTER ELEVEN

Isa took off her coat before sliding into the booth across from Mara, grateful to be out of Raptor Aeronautical while everything was going down. She hadn't seen Mara since Monday night anyway.

In the past few days Isa, Graysen, and Emerson had been very busy. Two people were being arrested today and another was being escorted out of the building for further questioning—and would likely be arrested. She didn't need to be around for that. Hamilton hadn't come out and said it, but she had a feeling a lot of people would put two and two together and realize that she was part of the reason people were getting arrested.

Mara smiled when she saw her. As usual she looked stunning in a simple green three-quarter-sleeve dress that matched her eyes. And her pixie-style haircut showed off her sharp cheekbones. "Hey, glad you made it. I ordered us an appetizer so I hope that's okay?"

"Of course. I'm starving. Today has been stressful." A fallout would follow from the two, potentially three, employees getting arrested, not to mention the fallout for their own families. After having her life ripped apart after her own father's sins, she couldn't help but feel bad for the immediate families of the people involved with stealing from the aeronautical company.

"I bet. How much longer will you be on this job? Or can you tell me that?"

"Another day or two, maybe." Which meant she might have to go in on Monday just to wrap up a few things, but this job had gone much quicker and smoother than predicted—and after Tuesday she didn't have to work with Graysen anymore so it was perfect timing. But there were a few more people she wanted to look into. Just for her peace of mind. She wanted to make sure when she and Graysen were gone that the company was as secure as it could be. At least from this point forward Raptor would be implementing new security measures overall.

"I know you can't tell me specifics, but this job seemed to stress you out more than normal." Concern glittered in her friend's green gaze.

"For more reasons than one." The other night she'd opened up to Mara about everything that had happened with Graysen a year ago. She was pretty sure that Mara already knew everything, considering the vetting process Isa'd had to go through when getting hired at Red Stone. Even if Mara didn't work for Red Stone, Isa thought maybe Harrison had said something. Either way, her friend had been very supportive when Isa had opened up to her.

"Yeah, I can imagine how hard it is to work with Graysen. Can I ask you something personal about him?"

She nodded, then paused to place her drink order with their waitress. When the woman was gone, Isa looked back at Mara. "You can ask anything you want."

"This is a nosy question and maybe I shouldn't even be asking it, so tell me to shut it, if so. You never said if he explained the specifics of his operation—why he did what he did where your...father was concerned." Compassion was clear in Mara's eyes and Isa knew her friend wasn't asking to be malicious.

Familiar pain tightened in Isa's chest. She hadn't talked about what happened with her father with anyone, really. After she lost all of her friends in DC it had been easy to shut everyone out Except for Mara. And she was really glad that she had opened up to the other woman.

"I know the basics of why my father was going to be arrested. But I didn't dig any deeper and...Graysen didn't tell me anything more than what the media reported." And every day since then it was hard for her to come to terms with the contrast between the man the media had portrayed her father as and the man she knew. The man who had sold state secrets was a monster, someone she couldn't imagine knowing.

Mara nodded, her lips pulling into a thin line. "I thought so. Look, I have some information for you. And I know I'm risking hurting our friendship by even bringing this up but I think you need to see it. For yourself, if you're ever going to heal. Some of this is classified, and those parts have been redacted, but everything else you'll be able to read. When you're done with the file you can give it back to me or burn it."

Isa had always wondered what Mara had done before marrying Harrison and getting heavily involved in charity work. Mara had been pretty vague, saying that she'd worked for the British government. Now Isa wondered even more if the woman had managed to get classified information. "You got this information on your own, or from Harrison?"

To her surprise Mara's cheeks flushed slightly. "Neither. I got it from my father-in-law. He pulled some strings. And fair warning, there are some graphic pictures in there. They're not pretty."

Isa could feel the blood drain from her cheeks, but didn't say anything as their waitress brought the appetizer and drinks. She ordered a small salad even though she wasn't remotely hungry anymore, mainly so the waitress would go away. "Will you tell me what's in the file before I open it?"

Mara's expression was grim. "There's information in there about exactly what your father did, and pictures of the people who got hurt because of his treachery."

Isa swallowed hard but nodded. She didn't see any judgment or recrimination on Mara's face. It was still difficult to talk about this with anyone, but if Mara thought she should look at the file, she would. She didn't trust many people anymore and her friend was one of the exceptions. "Okay, I'll read it."

Mara lifted a black and gray wool coat off the bench next to her to reveal a simple black purse that was more a shoulder bag than anything. She unzipped it and pulled out a fairly thick manila file. She paused for a moment then slid it across the table. "Wait until you're home to read this."

Nodding because her throat was too tight to talk, Isa took the file and slid it into her own purse.

"Is it okay that I brought this up?" Mara asked, concern in her eyes.

Somehow Isa found her voice, and nodded. "It is. It's just hard to talk about." Unless she was mentally prepared for it—which was pretty much never.

She felt as if the file was burning a hole in her purse, and it took all of her self-control not to whip the thing out and see what was inside. But she got through lunch and made it back to her temporary office to find Graysen waiting for her.

Things between them had been awkward since he'd showed up at her place on Monday, and she could admit that she'd been avoiding him most of the week whenever she could.

When she found him leaning against the window of her office, staring out at downtown, she tensed. "Is everything okay?" she asked as he turned to face her.

She'd noticed that there had only been a handful of people in their offices on this floor.

He nodded. "Yes. Hamilton called a company meeting to discuss all of the arrests today. That's why it's like a ghost town."

Nonetheless, she shut the door behind her in case anyone was around and might eavesdrop. "I still plan to go through more employee files this afternoon and tomorrow." She wanted to make sure that they crossed all their t's and dotted their i's. "Was there something specific you wanted to talk about?"

His shoulders were tense, his blue eyes unreadable. For a moment she thought he was going to say yes, but he shook his head. "No."

When he strode for the door she realized he didn't plan to say anything more. Maybe he had just come here to see her.

It pleased her and broke her heart at the same time. She hated this giant divide between them because...she'd never gotten over him. Even if she wanted to deny it, that was a simple truth. Michael or Graysen, she'd fallen hard for the man. Even with all his lies, they'd shared so many intimate moments that made her feel as if... She sighed, the ache in her chest spreading outward, making it hard to breathe for a moment. It didn't matter. Nothing would ever fix what was broken between them.

It made it harder, knowing he'd jump back into a relationship with her if she said the word. She ached to call out to him, to stop him from leaving, but she had no idea what to say.

Once he was gone she collapsed into her chair and placed her head in her hands. After taking a couple deep breaths she opened her bag and started to pull out her laptop but paused, and plucked the manila file out instead.

She should be working. Probably shouldn't even be looking at this, whatever it was. Mara had told her to wait until she was home and alone, but her curiosity wouldn't let her leave it.

* * *

Isa's fingers flew across the keyboard. She was trying to focus on work, but was having a hard time concentrating after reading that file Mara had given her. After seeing the pictures of some of the people who'd been killed because of her father's greed... Nope. Isa swallowed hard and mentally shook herself even as she cursed her trembling fingers.

Taking a deep breath, she stopped typing for a moment. If she allowed herself to dwell on what she'd read earlier she wouldn't be able to do her job. And Red Stone and the clients who hired them deserved better. She should have waited like Mara told her to. Curiosity had gotten the better of her.

Later tonight she would try to digest everything she'd learned. Though she had a feeling it would take a very long time to come to terms with the truth of who her father had been. A year later and she still couldn't quite deal. Now with even more information about the depth of his treachery... She rolled her shoulders once and ordered herself to focus on the present. Soon enough she'd talk to Graysen about what she'd learned today. She couldn't think about that though.

After the busy afternoon they'd had here, she still had more research to do, namely following the trail of emails and other projects Shawn Grady had worked on. Grady was one of the people who'd been escorted out of the building today, but not arrested. Not yet that she knew of, anyway. The other two, Gina Scott and Roy Winston, had been the ones arrested.

But Grady had been one of the people who'd accessed her laptop when he thought no one was around. It turned out that he'd planted tracking software into her laptop so that he could shadow her movements. Graysen had caught the man on video in her office and Isa had quickly figured out what Grady had done to her computer.

But after looking at his financials, it didn't appear as if he was stealing money or information. Which meant she needed to dig deeper into him. If he'd planted that software on her computer it was for a specific reason. Maybe he'd just been better at hiding his trail than the other two. She was determined to find out why he'd wanted to know what she was up to.

Emerson was currently working on the same thing so Isa had no doubt they'd figure out what this guy had been up to soon enough.

As she started looking deeper into Grady's emails, she frowned when she saw a couple from the VP of the company. Looking back through Grady's email history, his communication with the VP was very rare, but then he'd received an email telling him that he was needed for an urgent meeting only an hour before he planted the software on Isa's computer? It could mean nothing—probably did—but she made a note of it. Sometimes the most benign things ended up mattering in her job.

Moving on from there, she did something she hadn't planned to do—she pulled up personnel files on Alan Persky, the VP of Raptor Aeronautical. There were a handful of people Hamilton had said to leave out of their investigation, including Persky.

After everything she'd found to date...yeah, that wasn't happening. Hamilton had hired Red Stone to investigate the company and that was what she was going to do.

But as soon as she was done today, she was going to ask Graysen to come over to her place tonight. After everything she'd read in that file, they needed to talk. There were some things he hadn't told her—things that would have made her more willing to talk to him a year ago. More open to forgiving him.

She simply couldn't understand why he hadn't given her what Mara had given her today. It certainly would have helped make his case for being forgiven.

For a moment, she stopped what she was doing and rubbed a hand over the back of her neck. She reached for the phone on the desk, tempted to call him. When she'd come back from lunch the security guard had been insistent she leave her cell phone with him.

After the arrests today and all the commotion, she knew Raptor was cracking down on security. And technically the security guard should have been insisting from the beginning that she leave her cell phone every time she entered the building. In her report, she'd already noted the lack of adherence to strict protocol.

Isa clenched her fingers around the phone, picked it up, but immediately put it back in its cradle. Now wasn't the time to talk to Graysen. Not about personal stuff, anyway. And she knew he was with Hamilton right now, going over more of Raptor's security issues. What she wanted to talk about could wait until they had privacy.

Flexing her fingers, she got back to work. But she was determined that tonight she and Graysen were going to have a serious talk. And maybe, just maybe...they had a future after all. She wanted to know the truth of why he'd withheld so much information for so long, was even withholding it now.

If not for Mara, she'd still be in the dark.

CHAPTER TWELVE

Icy fingers of unease danced up Isa's spine as she packed up her laptop. She tried calling Graysen using the landline, but his cell phone went straight to voicemail. Maybe his phone was downstairs too, or maybe he was still in a meeting with Hamilton.

She doubted it, considering how late it was. She'd been in the zone for the last three hours, downloading information to her laptop and a backup flash drive which she'd securely tucked into the pocket of her pencil skirt. It was well past seven and she should have been out of here a couple hours ago. But once she'd started digging into Persky, she hadn't been able to stop. The information she'd found had her edgy and desperate to get it out of the building. But she needed to tell someone what she had first. For all she knew, she was wrong about what she'd found and it was nothing, but...her gut told her otherwise.

Since Graysen hadn't answered her, she peeked out into the hallway. The place was empty so she shut her door and immediately dialed Emerson. Her friend and coworker picked up on the second ring.

"Emerson here."

"Hey, it's me. I'm calling from a landline." She cleared her throat and looked around even though Graysen had personally checked this office for recording devices other than their own and found none. She knew no one was watching her. "Listen, I found some really strange information. I've downloaded everything and I'm heading out of here now. Where are you?"

"At the office still."

"I'm coming over right now. Wait for me, okay?"

"Of course. Is everything okay?"

"Ah, yeah. Have you talked to Graysen lately?"

"No. I tried calling him a while ago and it's going straight to voicemail. Need me to ping his phone, find out where he is?"

"No...ah, yes." Isa needed to talk to him too. She hated that she couldn't just email the files to Emerson but she wasn't able to send such sensitive information over regular email. And she couldn't trust a file hosting service either. It was against Red Stone protocol and Raptor Aeronautical's protocol to send or upload any classified information that way.

Considering the business Raptor did with the government, she understood why they had the security measures in place. And there was a chance the information she wanted to send—specs for military drones—could be seen by the wrong people. Hell, this was the kind of information even *she* didn't want access to. Now that she had it, however, she needed someone with more knowledge than her to look at the files. Since Emerson was part of the team working on this job and was by far the most tech-savvy person Isa knew other than Lizzy Caldwell, it made sense to give her a crack at the files. But she'd be calling her boss on the way to the office to let him know about this as well. She'd be looping everyone necessary into this.

"Give me a sec." There was a flurry of typing in the background, then, "The location of his phone is the lobby of Raptor."

Isa let out a short curse. "So's mine. He's not there." But at least it meant he was in the building. Or she assumed it did. She couldn't imagine him leaving his phone behind.

"What's going on?"

"Ah, I'm not sure. Maybe nothing." Feeling completely paranoid and not caring, she kept her words vague, not wanting to say too much over the phone.

The information she'd found had the VP's digital fingerprints all over the files she'd discovered. As if he'd tried to hide some of the records he'd had access to. He'd done a good job, but she'd been doing this kind of work for a long time, knew exactly what to look for. If she hadn't specifically been looking for anything out of the ordinary, however, she wouldn't have found it.

"I used to work for a tech company that had a strong focus in work effectiveness. I was trained well and I can read code on a basic level and…" She lowered her voice even though her door was shut and she was almost certain she was the only one left on this floor for the day. "There's something wrong with some of the files I came across. Odd-looking code has been input into places it shouldn't be. It's subtle and maybe I'm wrong but…I don't think so. Unfortunately, I don't know what any of it *means*." She just knew it shouldn't be there. She really hoped she was just being paranoid and that it was nothing.

"Okay, head over here now. I won't leave."

"I'll be there in about...ah, fifteen minutes. Maybe twenty. I've got to grab my cell phone downstairs then I'm gone." She wanted to wait to talk to Graysen first, but she needed to get this information out of the building and into the right hands. If anyone could understand this information, it would be Emerson. The woman was brilliant.

"I'll be waiting for you," Emerson said.

Once they disconnected she slid her laptop into her bag. The hallway seemed unusually quiet as she strode down toward the elevators, but she figured that was just her own nerves at what she'd found.

It was weird being so disconnected without her cell phone. Maybe that was why she was feeling so tense. Halfway down the hallway, the lights went off.

Instinctively she froze. Rolling her eyes at her jumpiness, she shook her head. The power going off was weird, but not unheard of. The city lights streamed into the hallway from multiple open doorways, giving her enough illumination to see, but it was so silent. Without the hum of computers, copy machines and everything else, it was beyond eerie.

Still, those icy fingers of unease she experienced earlier intensified as she realized that she could see lights from other buildings. Which meant it wasn't a general blackout. She ducked into the nearest office and strode to the huge window. Every building she could see downtown was brightly lit up. When she picked up the landline of whoever's office this was, there was no dial tone.

So the power in this building went off, as well as access to the phones, and it wasn't storming out? All the alarms in her head went off.

She didn't want to panic and read too much into this, but if it had something to do with what she'd found, she needed to get the hell out of here right now, cell phone or not. For all she knew someone had been listening to her phone conversation. It seemed unlikely, since Graysen had personally checked her office, but...he'd been busy today. They all had. Maybe something had slipped past them.

She inwardly cursed. Maybe she shouldn't have made that call to Emerson at all. But she'd wanted *someone* to know what she'd found before she left the building. As she headed back to the open doorway she paused at the sound of male voices.

Because she was feeling paranoid, she ducked behind the door instead of announcing her presence. She knew she was probably being stupid, but she'd rather laugh at herself later than make a mistake. Breathing unevenly, she looked through the crack of the half-open door.

Muted footsteps strode down the hall at a steady pace.

"She should be up here," a quiet male voice said.

She?

Anxiety slithered through Isa at his words. As far as she knew she was the only person here right now. The floor was very large, however, so maybe—

Her gut tightened as two men holding pistols at their sides slowly moved past the doorway. It took her all of two seconds to realize there were silencers on the end of both of their guns. Otherwise the weapons wouldn't be so long. Beads of sweat rolled down her spine.

What the ever-loving hell was going on?

She didn't allow herself even a breath of relief as they kept going. Hell no, she was in danger and needed to get out of here like ten minutes ago. She slowly reached into her bag, palmed her keys and clutched them tightly so they wouldn't jingle. With a shaking hand, she managed to tuck them into the tight pocket of her skirt. She still had the flash drive in her other pocket. At least the keys wouldn't make any noise. Next she slid her laptop out of her bag and eased her bag to the ground. She didn't need it to weigh her down right now and there was no way she was leaving her laptop behind for someone to find.

Listening to the sound of their soft footfalls, she waited until she thought they were far enough down the hallway away from her to peek out the doorway. When she looked, she saw two shadowy figures stepping into her temporary office.

Heart racing, she knew it was now or never. She slipped out of her heels, tucked them behind the door with her bag and ran down the hallway as fast and as quietly as she could manage. Her pulse was out of control, the sound of her heartbeat thudding in her ears so loudly she was glad she was the only one who could hear it.

She needed to put as much distance between her and them as possible. She didn't care who they were or who had sent them. All she knew was that two men with guns were looking for her.

Just as she was about to reach the end of the hallway where it T-boned into the elevators, she heard a shout behind her.

"Hey!" one of the men yelled.

No way was Isa going to respond or turn around and slow down. Since the elevators wouldn't be working without power, she veered left toward the stairs. Now she didn't bother to mute her movements, and ran as fast as she could.

She slammed her hands into the metal release bar. The door flew open, ricocheting off the wall. At this point it didn't matter how loud she was. She was running for her life.

The sound of her heart pounding in her ears was all she could hear as she entered the dimly lit stairwell. There was an orange glow barely illuminating her way, probably from a generator or something. She wasn't sure if she should try hiding somewhere or just run. In the end she made the decision to run. She didn't have a choice, not when two men wanted to kill her—or maybe they wanted to kidnap and torture her. Either option wasn't good. Because she was pretty sure they didn't just want to talk to her.

The concrete and metal of the stairs was cold against the soles of her bare feet as she made her way down flight after flight. Sweat slicked the back of her neck and down her spine, the fear punching through her, needle-sharp. She alternated between feeling hot and cold. As she made it down another flight, she heard a door slam open from above. It had to be the two men.

Instead of continuing racing downstairs, she stopped at the nearest door and opened it as quietly as she could. She slipped into the hallway of the sixth floor and gently pulled the door shut behind her. She could only hope they wouldn't realize she'd exited the stairwell here.

Her feet were silent along the carpeted hallway and she was grateful for the downtown light helping to illuminate her way. There were so many shadows though, and she was terrified there were more men waiting in them, ready to shoot her. She wished she had a better plan other than to put distance between the two men with guns and find a way to call for help if she couldn't get out of the building. But that was all she could do right now. She also desperately needed to get in contact with Graysen, to make sure he was okay. But she had no idea how the hell to do that, not when his phone was in the lobby. *One step at a time*, she ordered herself. She was going to find a way to call for help no matter what.

Halfway down the hall, she heard a woman talking. On instinct she sidestepped into what turned out to be a copy room.

"Generator…"

"We'll figure it out…" That was definitely a male voice.

Straining, struggling to keep her breathing under control, she tried to listen harder and figure out who the two people were and whether she knew them. For all she knew they were with the men who were running after her.

When the voices got closer, she squeezed behind one of the copy machines. Because there wasn't much light, she was able to use the shadows to help her remain invisible.

She tensed when a woman screamed and a man shouted. What the hell was going on out there? Torn between leaving her hiding space or staying there, her decision was made when she heard a *puff, puff, puff* of air. The screaming and shouting immediately cut off.

Oh, God. Isa bit down on the inside of her lip. They'd shot those people.

Hot tears stung her eyes. Two innocent people were dead. Or dying.

"Damn it... Not the right woman." The man's voice was frustrated and way too close for comfort. She couldn't see but it sounded like he was near the doorway of the copy room or just inside it.

She barely breathed, too afraid to make any noises.

"What should we do with the bodies?" another man asked.

Ohgodohgodohgod. She had no weapon and no way to call anyone for help. All she could hope was that Graysen wasn't in the same situation she was. Of course if he was, he was a heck of a lot more trained than she was to deal with armed men.

"Have someone clean up tonight. Or maybe leave them. I don't know what the plan is but it's not our problem..." His words trailed off and she heard a tapping sound. She couldn't figure out what it was.

"Come on, let's keep sweeping."

"Even if the stupid bitch makes it downstairs she won't get out of here alive." The second man made an obnoxious snorting sound.

She forced herself to stay where she was, and counted to sixty seconds as they moved away from the copy room. Then she counted to sixty again, and again, until ten full minutes had passed.

Even though she was terrified to move from her hiding place, she knew she had to. She couldn't stay here and wait for them to come back. No, she had to get help, find a phone, something. Her knees ached as she pushed up and wiggled out of her hiding spot. Thankfully no one was waiting to attack her. As she stepped into the middle of the room, two legs became visible through the doorway. A three-inch heel dangled from one of the woman's feet and the other shoe was a foot away from her body.

Clutching her laptop tightly to her chest, Isa peered out into the hallway. Now she could see the woman's entire body, and a man not far from her, sprawled on his back. A big stain spread across the man's shirt, and in the dimness it looked black. But she knew what it was. His blood.

Her skin crawled. Just to be sure she tested their pulses, even if there was nothing she could do for them. But both of them were dead. Then, feeling ghoulish, she checked them for cell phones just in case. Nothing.

As one of the killers' words replayed in her mind, she tried to figure out her next move. He'd said if she made it downstairs, she still wouldn't escape. There had to be more of them, or someone else waiting for her.

Think, think, think.

Graysen was well-trained, and if he was in the building would know what to do. She needed to find him somehow, and the only thing she could think to do at this point was to return to her office. She'd already been there so those men likely wouldn't return. At least not right away. Eventually they'd do another full sweep and if they had enough men, they'd find her. She had to get help before that happened.

But maybe Graysen had gone looking for her—she hoped so. If he wasn't there, she would head to the office they'd been using during the week to view the video footage.

If he wasn't in either of those places, she'd figure out what to do then. For now, she would take things one step at a time and just try to stay alive.

Though she hated to use the stairs, there was no other way around it. Instead of using the stairwell on the west side, however, she headed to the east stairwell.

Taking a deep breath, she eased the door open. She couldn't hear any movement and there was just the faintest light illuminating the stairwell. It would have to do.

Her feet were silent once again as she raced up the stairs. And once more all she could hear was the pounding of her heart. This was a nightmare come to life. She'd never felt so vulnerable. Not even the day she'd seen her father's body sprawled on the floor. She just prayed that Graysen was okay.

The thought of something happening to him terrified her. It didn't matter what had happened in their past. In this moment, she desperately wanted him to be alive and well. If anyone could survive, it would be him. And he would help her.

Still holding her laptop in a death grip with one hand, she wiped her free damp palm on her skirt as she reached the tenth floor. Sucking in a quiet breath, she pulled the door open a crack so she could peer into the hallway.

Shadows and muted streams of outside city lights from open doorways greeted her.

When a door from somewhere below her groaned open, she darted into the hallway. As the door shut quietly behind her, a big hand slammed over her mouth.

CHAPTER THIRTEEN

Alan paced back and forth in the lobby. Everything had gone so incredibly wrong. Luckily Yuri thought they could still salvage this operation, but too many people were dead to cover this up now.

Which meant they were going to have to make this look like a terrorist attack—and technically it was.

"Stop worrying. We have this under control." The man named Dmitri spoke quietly, not moving from his position by the security desk in the lobby. His dark eyes were like black pools.

Unease crawled up his spine. Alan wouldn't admit it, but the man and everyone else Yuri had sent in tonight scared him. It was probably a good thing Yuri himself wasn't here. "I'm not worried," he snapped.

But…he was. When he'd overheard Isa Harper's phone conversation with a woman named Emerson a half hour ago, he'd gone into panic mode. He'd tapped Isa's phone so he'd know exactly what she was up to. He was worried that he might have overreacted, but something about her tone had bothered him. Not to mention the Emerson woman had mentioned pinging someone named Graysen via the man's phone. And that phone was supposed to be in this lobby. It was too late now to worry about it since everything was set into motion.

Alan had already gone through the phones left with security but all of them had security codes so he couldn't get into them. Not that it mattered. Once Alan had heard that conversation, he'd contacted Yuri—who'd immediately activated his reinforcements: a dozen trained men who'd been waiting in two vans in the parking garage of the building.

Alan had known they were there, of course. The men had been hiding for the past two days. He'd given them security passes to get into the garage and building. No one, not even security, had any idea that armed men had been waiting in those vans.

Alan had only wanted to contain Isa and find out what she knew, if anything, before killing her. He hadn't wanted to kill anyone else in the building. But when she'd said she'd found some files with odd-looking code, he'd had to act fast and get the building contained before she could send anything out or make any more calls. It had to be the files with the specs for the military drones. He wasn't directly involved with the project but he'd modified Raptor's programming. He'd been so damn careful but she must have found something.

Now everything was a giant clusterfuck since too many people were dead. And Alan wanted to know who the hell the man named Graysen was that Isa had referred to. If he had to guess, it was the new hire Hamilton had brought in. Not that he could very well ask Hamilton. The man had gone home for the evening, and as far as Alan was concerned, he was going to come to work tomorrow just like everyone else and find out that their company had been robbed and most of the security guys killed. To cover his bases, Alan had made everyone on the security team who had families call home and tell them they'd be working late so no worried spouse would call the cops. Then Dmitri had killed them. That was one thing he didn't have to worry about.

Yuri had rerouted the alert that should have gone to Hamilton when the power had gone out so he never received it. Another thing taken care of. Still... Sweat beaded at the base of Alan's spine as he thought of everything else that could go wrong.

Yuri had a plan in place to frame it on two of their current single security guys—the two men had been killed but their bodies would never be found. Alan had no idea what was going to happen to the bodies, and he didn't much care as long as they disappeared. Yuri was going to leave a paper trail making it look like they'd fled the country late tonight.

Raptor Aeronautical had many patents, so framing the two men for stealing the information and selling it to the highest bidder wouldn't be hard to believe. Alan just hated that things had gotten so messy. This was supposed to have been controlled, with no one knowing anything out of the ordinary had happened here until long afterward. When he put in his notice with the company, he'd wanted it to be without any cloud hanging above him. He might still be able to pull off this op, but the timing of his leaving the company after an attack wasn't ideal.

Alan frowned at Dmitri when he let out a curse.

"What is it?" he asked as Dmitri shoved his phone into the pocket of his tactical pants.

"Two of my men are dead."

He stiffened. "What? How?" The people who worked here were analysts, techs, and computer types. Even the former military hires they had were all intel people. Not highly trained soldiers. And he'd seen the resume of every single person who'd been hired, so he knew that for a fact. The company's security people were all accounted for. Either dead or currently incapacitated by Yuri's people.

"Broken necks." Dmitri's expression was grim and slightly accusing as he stared at Alan.

"You think I know who did that?" He could feel sweat beading his upper lip and across his forehead. Nothing was going according to plan. And he wouldn't be paid the rest of his money until everything was delivered. His fiancée wouldn't like that. She was so insistent they live a certain lifestyle.

He rolled his shoulders, forced himself to think. He'd already input the last of the special code into the final design for the military drones they were releasing to the American government soon.

It had been woven in so subtly to the onboard computers, it was practically invisible. No one would discover what he'd done. Or they shouldn't have been able to discover it. Unfortunately he was afraid Isa had. That was why he had to make sure she didn't make it out of the building.

Once those drones crossed the border into certain areas, Yuri and the people he worked for would be able to commandeer the drones easily. From there...Alan didn't care what they did with them.

That wasn't his problem. The only thing he cared about was making sure that bitch Isa didn't get out of the building alive. And now apparently they needed to find whoever had killed two of Yuri's men and make sure they didn't get out either—because he somehow doubted Isa had broken the necks of two of Yuri's men. He supposed it was possible, but she didn't look strong enough.

"Has anyone made a call to the police?" Alan asked, since Yuri's people were monitoring local police communication.

Dmitri shook his head. "No. You have no idea who could have killed my men?" His dark eyes were murderous as he stared at Alan.

He blinked at the accusatory tone. "No." He wanted his damn money, wanted to leave the country.

Dmitri just gave him another hard look before turning away from him. He shouted out orders to three of his men who immediately headed for one of the stairwells. Alan wasn't certain what he said since he spoke in Russian, but it was pretty damn clear Dmitri had ordered them to find whoever had done this.

The only reason Alan wasn't completely panicking right now was because the building was locked down and there was no way for Isa to communicate with anyone outside it. That was why they had to make sure she didn't make it out of here alive.

If he could leave, he would. But if tried he knew that Dmitri would kill him. He might have already input all the code but he only got paid once those drones were delivered. So they had to make sure absolutely no one was suspicious of the drone project.

He was tempted to simply run and just try to live on the money he'd already made. He and his fiancée would be able to make do... But for now, he planned to see this through to the end. Once Isa and whoever her partner was were killed, he and Yuri's team would all leave the building.

Then in the morning he'd come to work and act just as shocked as everyone else by the massacre that had occurred here. He'd have to deal with questions from the police, and yeah, probably the Feds, but he'd go through with it, appear shaken and distraught.

Nothing that happened here should be traceable back to him. Most importantly, no one would even know the drone project had been compromised. The authorities would be looking for the terrorists who'd attacked the building and stolen the patent to Project ACAS—an important project for the company, but with no ties to him.

He just had to get through the next few hours alive—and make sure Isa Harper didn't.

CHAPTER FOURTEEN

"It's me," Graysen said quietly as Isa reared her head back, trying to slam it against his face.

Immediately she stilled and he let his hand drop from her mouth. He'd been ready to kill whoever had come through that door, to snap their neck—until he'd realized it was her.

She swiveled, fear clear in her expression even under the dim lighting. She opened her mouth to speak but he just held up a finger and pointed down the hallway.

She nodded and he stepped in front of her, wanting to be between her and any more potential threats. He wasn't certain what was going on yet, but this building was under attack. He'd already killed two armed men with Russian tattoos. If he'd had his cell phone or camera, he'd have snapped some images of the tats.

Moving quickly down the hallway, he was aware of Isa directly behind him. Her scent and heat practically wrapped around him, reminded him she was *alive*. The sheer relief he experienced when he realized it was her stepping out into the hallway, that she was unharmed... There were no words to describe how he felt now. All he knew was that he was going to make sure he got her out of this alive.

Whatever the hell *this* was.

He'd left a meeting with Hamilton an hour ago and had been doing some work in one of the offices when the power went out. When he'd noticed that the building was the only one in the city that appeared to have lost power, he'd gone to find Isa.

Instead he'd found two armed men roaming the halls. Two armed men with *suppressors* on their Gen3 Glocks. He'd quickly taken care of the problem—then divested them of their weapons. But he still wasn't certain what he and Isa were up against.

The building was square-shaped, with the hallways running in a perfect square and offices on the interior and exterior. On the fourth floor there was a walkway that attached to a neighboring parking garage owned and used by Raptor Aeronautical. He had no doubt the main entrance to the parking garage was being guarded. But there was another way into the garage, one exclusively used by Hamilton.

The only reason he knew about it was because of the CEO himself. Unfortunately, there was still a chance it was being guarded as well, but at this point they had very few options for getting out of the building unnoticed. If he could just call in for backup, he had no doubt they'd be able to hole up somewhere until then.

Without knowing more about who had this building under siege or how far they were willing to go to flush out anyone inside, his options were limited.

When they came to an office on the opposite side of the building from the elevators, he ducked inside, Isa right behind him. He shut the door and turned to face her, taking in her appearance fully. No shoes, which he'd already noticed, but she seemed unharmed.

"Have you been hurt?"

"No. But they killed two people, a man and a woman." Her voice trembled slightly, but she was holding up well.

"I saw the bodies." He'd nearly lost his mind when he'd seen the motionless female body. For a moment he'd thought it was Isa and... He couldn't even go there.

She swallowed hard before continuing. "I think I know why this is happening. I found something in the specs for military drones about to be released to the US government in the next week—in the actual computer programming. I know I wasn't even supposed to be looking in those files, but I followed a hunch. I have no idea what the actual code means but it shouldn't *be* there. I called Emerson from a landline because I didn't have my cell... This is all my fault. What I said shouldn't have been enough for all this." She motioned with her hand, her voice low. "But I don't believe in coincidence. This has to be because of that phone conversation. Alan Persky is the man I found linked to the code. He tried to cover his tracks and did a damn good job, but I was digging hard."

Persky, the VP of the company. Yeah, he'd have unlimited access to pretty much *everything*. Still, the man would have left a digital trail no matter how hard he tried to hide it. Graysen could see by the recrimination in Isa's expression that she blamed herself for what was going on, but now wasn't the time to reassure her. "You saved all the information?"

"Yeah, on my laptop." She held it out for him and rattled off what name she'd saved the files as.

He snagged it from her, slid it out from the soft case and turned it on. This was a Red Stone laptop, one she'd used specifically for this op. They'd been monitoring it, and had left a security lock off it so sneaky employees up to no good would be tempted to look at her computer. It was the reason they'd managed to get two people arrested today. And soon, likely a third. Not that it mattered right now.

As soon as the laptop fired up, he tried to hook up to a wireless connection. They might not have any power here, but he was hopeful they could connect to a neighboring building. He knew the chances were slim, but he had to try.

"I also saved the information on a flash drive," Isa whispered as he tried to find an unsecured connection.

"Good," he murmured, typing quickly. If he could get a message out to Harrison, they'd be home free.

She started rummaging through the desk drawers. Without asking, he knew what she was doing: looking for a cell phone. *Smart woman.*

"Damn it." Of course there were no unsecured connections in the business district. But he'd been hoping to find a random coffee shop or something with free Wi-Fi. From their location, however, he couldn't connect to anyone. With enough time he could probably hack into someone's system, but right now they didn't have time.

He shut the laptop and looked up at her. "I set up an email to automatically send to Harrison as soon as this computer connects to the internet."

"So what you're saying is, if we don't make it out of here alive, if we get this laptop somewhere secure, the message will eventually make it to Harrison?"

He nodded. "That's the plan."

"Good. Where do you want to leave it?" she asked.

He scrubbed a hand over the back of his neck. One laptop in a huge building would be difficult to locate no matter how many people they had sweeping the place.

"There's a possibility that Hamilton has a cell phone in his office. I spotted a satellite phone on his desk earlier in the week." And leaving the laptop there would be as good a place as any. Not to mention Hamilton had a private stairwell, one that led to the parking garage. Unfortunately, his office was on the top floor.

"We'll have to get up the rest of the stairs undetected." Isa's voice was grim.

He nodded again. "I know. I've got two weapons I took off two men I killed."

Her eyes widened. "Wait...where are the bodies?"

"I dragged them into an office." He hadn't had time to hide them well, not when his main focus had been finding Isa.

She let out a short curse. "Whoever is working with Persky is going to find out soon enough—if they haven't already."

He nodded. "Exactly. And staying in one spot is stupid. We need to be on the move, trying to find a way out of here. I think Hamilton's office is a good spot to start." At the very least they could hide the laptop there while they tried to find a way out. If not through the parking garage, then they'd find another way. Or if they had to, they could just hole up there as long as they could. He had two weapons, which wasn't a lot against an unknown number of enemies.

She nodded after a long moment. "If he doesn't have a satellite phone, we can keep searching for cell phones in other offices."

"Agreed." His voice was low, and even though now wasn't the time, he gently cupped her cheek, needing the contact with her. "I'm glad you're okay."

"I'm glad you are too." She placed her hand over his in a gentle hold, the action mirroring the surprising tenderness he saw in her gaze.

Though it jarred him, there was no time to dwell on it. He dropped his hand and pulled out one of the pistols. He knew she could shoot well, thanks to the training her father had made sure she had. Isa might not like weapons but he wanted her to have one now.

He handed it to her and though he could see slight distaste in her eyes she nodded and took it. She held it against her body and kept her finger off the trigger.

He pulled out the other weapon, and automatically checked to see how many rounds it held even though he'd checked before. Force of habit. "We're going to head to the eastern stairwell. From there we'll go as far as we can. If we hear someone entering the stairwell, we take the closest exit." Graysen had no doubt of his own skill, but he didn't want to put Isa in any unnecessary danger. If that meant lying low instead of facing some of these threats head on, that was the way it had to be. "We'll avoid using these weapons if at all possible." Because he wanted to save ammunition in case they got trapped somewhere. But he didn't tell her that.

She nodded and reached for the laptop, but he picked it up and tucked it into the back of his pants. It was slim enough that it fit fine against him.

"If I tell you to run, you run. Got it?" He needed to know that she would follow orders. There were too many unknowns, and with such a huge threat, he had to be secure in her reactions.

"I'll do whatever you say. You're the trained one."

His gaze fell to her mouth and he had the most insane urge to kiss her. He wouldn't. The timing was pure shit and she wouldn't welcome him anyway, but the urge was still there. It would probably never go away.

He nodded and turned away from her. Quietly, he opened the door a fraction, listening for any sounds. After ten solid seconds and hearing nothing, he drew his weapon and swept out into the hallway. It was empty in both directions. Turning, he motioned to Isa, who hurried out behind him.

She might be a civilian, but she was holding up incredibly well. After everything she'd been through a year ago, he wasn't surprised. Even if he hated that she was stuck here with him right now. He would do anything to get her to safety.

Their movements were mostly silent as they hurried down the hallway. Her breathing was slightly elevated, the only giveaway that she was stressed. When they neared the end of that first hallway he held up a hand and slowed, motioning for her to do the same.

A slight shuffling made him pause. Then he heard it again. When he turned to Isa, saw her eyes had widened, he knew she'd heard it too. He pointed to a doorway with the door cracked open about a foot.

He waited until she'd slipped inside then put a finger over his lips. She nodded but he saw her surprise when he shut the door, closing her inside. He wanted to know she was somewhere relatively hidden while he did some recon.

Someone was trying to be quiet, which could mean another innocent civilian was trapped in the building, or one of Persky's men was hunting for him and Isa. He was betting on the latter. There weren't that many people in the building around this time of night on a regular basis.

With his back against the wall at the end of the hallway, he kept completely immobile, strained to listen.

He heard the shuffling again. Then again. It was very faint, like the sound of clothing rustling. Maybe someone was sweeping offices. Or some innocent civilian stuck in the building had witnessed some of the bloodshed and was attempting to hide. Didn't matter. He needed to find out if there was a threat coming his and Isa's way.

He ducked into the office next to the one Isa was hiding in. He had to trust that she would stay put. She was smart and wanted to get out of this alive as much as he did.

She sure as hell wouldn't be safe forever, so he had to make sure no one got through him. He would keep her safe, no matter what.

He left the door slightly ajar and hid behind it. Using the shadows as cover, he kept an eye on the corner of the hallway so he'd see when anyone rounded the corner. From the sound of it, someone was definitely coming their way.

Adrenaline pumped through him as he honed his focus. But training and instinct wouldn't allow him to zero in only on that potential entry for a threat. He was very aware that someone could come up on him from behind. Unfortunately, that was a risk he was willing to take. Anything to keep Isa safe.

The tenderness he'd seen in her gaze earlier was still with him. He couldn't get the sight of it out of his head. She'd looked at him the way she had when they'd been a couple. When he'd been lying to her about who he really was.

He might have missed her desperately for the past year, but seeing that expression on her face was like a punch to his solar plexus. A reminder of everything he'd lost.

All the muscles in his body tightened when he saw one man, then another, both armed, round the corner. He'd been right—the slight shuffling he'd heard was their clothing. They were quiet enough, but without any external noise like the hum of lights or computers, every sound seemed over-pronounced right now. Which was why he would have to move hard and fast.

He needed to take both these threats out without any fanfare. He hoped there were only two of them. The two men who Isa had seen earlier had been working as a team. And the two men he'd killed had been working as a team as well.

It stood to reason there were only two men here now if they stuck to pattern. But if there were more, he'd end them too. He'd end anyone who thought they could harm Isa.

He waited one beat, then two. Three, four. They moved farther into the hallway, almost past his line of sight. He didn't see anyone else coming. Had to move now, regardless. They were sweeping offices and his would be one of the first.

He watched from the shadows as one man made a hand motion to his partner, showing that they'd split up—one going into the office across the hall, while this guy would move to the one Graysen was in.

Whisper silent, Graysen stepped out, his weapon already raised. He shot the one closest first, then the next. It took 1.5 seconds to make the head shots. The second guy had started to raise his weapon but he never got the chance to fire. Graysen didn't bother checking their pulses. No one survived a head shot.

Keeping his weapon up, he scanned the hallway behind him before easing around the corner the men had come from. He couldn't afford to get sloppy now.

There were a hell of a lot of shadows but it appeared clear. And it was silent.

Moving quickly, he dragged the two bodies into the office he'd been hiding in. Nothing to do about the blood stains on the carpet or against the wall, but at least it put the men out of sight. He patted them down, found no cell phones.

Of course it couldn't be that easy. But he did take their weapons: two more Glocks, again with suppressors, and three blades between them. He was actually glad for the suppressors since no one would be alerted about the shots he'd just made.

He also stripped them from the waist up when he realized they had on Kevlar vests. Took both of them. Then he snagged both hand-held radios, hooked one onto his belt.

Once he'd taken everything from them he and Isa could possibly use, he gave two gentle knocks on the door of the office she was in. They might not have a signal in place but he hoped she wouldn't shoot someone who took the time to knock.

He stepped inside, found it empty. "It's me, Isa."

She popped up from behind the desk, her eyes wide. In the dimness, her normally bright green eyes appeared to be almost black. "I heard a couple thuds. Are you okay?"

"Fine. I took out two of them. Come on, we need to get moving." As she rounded the desk, he held out one of the vests for her. "It wouldn't hurt to wear this. And this," he said, handing her a pair of socks he'd taken from one of the dead men. Her feet had to be hurting by now.

Wordlessly, she slipped the vest on over her head as he did the same with his, tightening the Velcro in places. It stood to reason that any armed men coming for them would aim for the head once they realized Isa and Graysen had on body armor, but accurate head shots were damn hard to make.

When they were done, he handed her the radio. She hooked it onto her skirt, but it was too heavy and slid off so he took it back. After a quick search of three offices, he found a duffle bag someone used for the gym, emptied the dirty clothes in it and dropped everything he'd taken into it—except the laptop, which he handed off to her. Then he hooked the long strap over his body and wore the bag like a satchel.

"You ready?"

A brisk nod, her expression determined. "Yeah."

After peering out and scanning the hallway again, he stepped out, Isa right with him. Adrenaline punched through him as they reached the next stairwell entrance. He motioned for her to stand flat against the wall as he pushed the release bar.

Weapon up, he eased the door open. No one was waiting to ambush them. He was still tense, all the muscles in his body pulled tight as he moved carefully onto the landing. Isa moved in behind him, held the door until it shut quietly.

He pointed upward even though she knew what they were doing. She just nodded. He could have moved faster, but kept pace with her as they headed up the stairs.

Even with the extra added weight of the Kevlar vest and no shoes she was still moving at an impressive clip. Fear of dying could do that to someone. They made it to the top floor in record time but Graysen was still careful as he opened it using the old-school key he'd received at the beginning of this job. Since he'd been on this floor before he knew the layout well.

Glossy tile gleamed under the city lights streaming in. He paused, listened. No signs of life.

Even so, he moved in first, weapon ready as he scanned the area. Hamilton's assistant's desk was clutter free and because it was glass and chrome it was clear no one was using it as a place to hide. Isa stepped in with him, her own pistol in hand.

She looked so damn fierce with the vest and weapon.

He motioned for her to stand next to a bookshelf on one of the walls of the huge, open space.

Methodically, he checked the visitors' restroom, then Hamilton's private one as well as his office before moving on to the conference rooms and other offices not currently in use. The entire floor had the feel of being empty but he had to be vigilant.

Once he was certain the floor was clear, he hurried back to Isa, gently took her elbow and led her to Hamilton's office. Inside, he shut the door and locked it for good measure as she set the laptop on the oversized desk. He did the same with the bag.

"How'd you get a key to Hamilton's office?" Isa asked, her voice still low even though there was enough insulation where they were that no one would be able to hear them.

Instead of answering, he crushed his mouth to hers, pushing her up against the nearest wall. The timing was shit, but he didn't care. There was a chance they weren't going to make it out of here, and if they didn't—he was going to taste her one more time.

She arched into him, grabbing onto his Kevlar vest and tugging him even closer as her lips clashed with his.

The hunger emanating from her was almost a tangible thing, her need matching his as she nipped at his bottom lip. He cupped the back of her head hard, some part of him afraid she'd pull back, and he simply wasn't done. Couldn't stop tasting, kissing her.

He felt like a man dying of thirst and she was his salvation. He hadn't realized how bland his life had been until she'd come into it a year ago. It had been even worse once she'd left him because he'd had a brief glimpse into what happiness was, only to have it ripped away.

The sane part of his brain knew they couldn't do this for long, that he couldn't be distracted. Using willpower he didn't know he had, he pulled back, breathing as hard as her.

"I'm not sorry for that," he rasped out, staring down at her beautiful face.

Her lips were swollen, her gaze slightly dazed. "I'm not either."

Good, he thought savagely. Very soon, they were going to do more than just kiss. If they made it out of here tonight, he was claiming her forever. After the way she'd reacted to him, she couldn't deny the chemistry that still burned between them.

There would never be anyone else for him. He knew that with a bone-deep certainty. He didn't care how long it took to convince her of the same.

Now he just had to make sure they got out of this alive. First thing on his agenda: finding that damn satellite phone.

CHAPTER FIFTEEN

Emerson stared at her cell phone. She'd already called Harrison, Grant, Porter, and Lizzy. No one was answering their phone. The only reason she could remotely think of for none of them answering was that there had been an emergency on another job. Still...one of them should be available. The only other reason she could think of was that Belle had gone into labor and things weren't going well. That thought made her pause.

She had no reason to call the police simply because Isa hadn't showed up to the Red Stone office like she said she would thirty minutes ago. Now Emerson had no way to get in contact with her. Every time she tried to call Raptor's main building, it went to a recorded voicemail. So her options were limited. But she couldn't let this go. It wasn't like Isa to flake on her. And even though she had been pretty vague when they'd talked last, something about her tone had been off. No, something had to be wrong.

Feeling only a little foolish, she decided to call Carlito. He was the first person she thought of and she knew he wouldn't make her feel stupid for being worried about her friend. The job she was working on with Isa and Graysen—whose phone was also still in the lobby of the Raptor Aeronautical building—was classified. While she couldn't tell Carlito specifics about the job, she could still ask him for an unofficial police escort. She'd feel better having someone go with her anyway and she trusted him.

Emerson tried to convince herself that once she got to Raptor she'd discover that Isa and Graysen had gotten tied up with work.

She couldn't even make herself believe the lie.

No matter what, she needed to see for herself that her friend was okay. And if Isa wasn't... No, she wouldn't think like that.

Carlito answered on the second ring. "Hey, I was just coming to see you."

Her heart stuttered just a little bit at the thought of him dropping by tonight to see her. "Are you nearby?"

"Yeah, about two minutes away."

"Do you feel like giving me a ride somewhere? Isa called me a while ago and was supposed to meet me here. But she hasn't shown up. And that's not like her. I think it might have something to do with the job we're working on. I can't really say more than that."

"No problem. But what did Harrison say?"

She let out a sigh even as she started closing down her computer and cleaning up her desk for the day. "I've tried calling everyone I can think of who has the clearance for this job and no one is answering. Do you know if Belle went into labor?"

"Oh hell, that's definitely a possibility. Last time I talked to Grant he said she was really close. Do you want me to see if I can get in touch with their dad?"

She paused as she closed her office door behind her. "Ah, yes, if you don't mind." Technically Keith Caldwell didn't work for the company anymore. He'd handed everything over to his sons, but he was the founder. She simply hadn't thought about calling him, however. "If you get in contact with him, will you ask him to have Harrison call me back?"

"No problem."

"Thanks. I'll be downstairs in a couple minutes."

"I'll pull right up to the front of the building."

"Okay, see you in a sec." She was already feeling better about going over to Raptor Aeronautical now that Carlito was here. Getting to spend a little extra time with Carlito? Not the worst thing in the world. Not even close.

Minutes later she strode through the lobby of Red Stone Security, waved at two of the security guys she knew, and stepped out into the cool December air.

Carlito was waiting at the curb in his big, dark blue truck. And no surprise to her, he jumped out when he saw her and opened the passenger door. The man certainly had manners. In fact, he was pretty damn perfect. She couldn't believe that it had taken her so long to realize that the sweetest man was right in front of her face and that she wanted way more than friendship with him.

"How serious do you think this thing with Isa is?" he asked, his expression pure cop mode, which she'd only seen a couple times before.

"Honestly, I'm not sure." She slid into the seat, was surprised when he leaned over to strap her in.

He did it so quickly, and there was nothing intimate about it, but having him so close to her made her light-headed for a moment. That masculine, familiar scent rolled over her, made her want to inhale deeper. But she didn't want to look crazy so she restrained herself.

He didn't respond until he'd slid into the driver's seat. "I turned on the seat warmer so if it gets too hot on your side just let me know." She was touched by his thoughtfulness, but before she could respond, he continued. "I couldn't get hold of Keith. So I think they must all be at the hospital. It's the only thing that makes sense. So when I ask how serious this is, what I'm saying is, should I call in backup right now?" He shot her an intent look as he stared down the quiet road in the business district.

"I don't think it's that serious. But..." She contemplated how much she could tell him without divulging anything classified. Emerson took her job seriously, but she needed to look out for her friends. "Today two people were arrested, thanks to the work we've done on this job—which is great news. And one was brought in for questioning. As far as I know he hasn't been arrested yet. We were planning on wrapping this job up by Monday or Tuesday at the latest. Then Isa called and she sounded a little off." And that was all she was comfortable saying.

"Okay." He nodded, looking thoughtful. "We'll park and head into the main lobby. I'll show my badge, and say I need to speak to one of their employees. How does that sound?"

Relief slid through Emerson's veins. "That sounds perfect. Oh, you'll need to ask for Isa Johnson, not Harper."

Carlito raised an eyebrow, but didn't comment. He cleared his throat as they reached a red light. "About that parade Saturday."

A sharp sense of disappointment threatened to overwhelm her. There was something foreboding in his tone, as if he was about to cancel on her. Maybe he really was seeing someone new and they had plans. She steeled herself for what he was about to say. "If you can't make it, it's okay."

He shot her a sharp look, his gray eyes piercing. "I'm going. I wanted to know if we were going as friends or as a date. For the record, I'm hoping you say the latter."

Her eyes widened as she digested his words. A brief honk from the vehicle behind them made her jump. He faced forward and pressed on the gas.

She stared at his profile, drinking in the sharp lines of his face as she forced her voice to work. "You want to go with me on a date?"

"Yep. I've wanted to ask you out for about six months."

She continued staring, digesting that as well. Carlito wanted to date her? *Um, yes, please.* "Are you talking casual dating?" Because she couldn't do that. Couldn't just be another woman he was seeing. It would carve her up inside. She was an all or nothing kind of girl.

He snorted, gave her another one of those heated looks that made her toes curl in her boots. "Fuck. No."

She jolted at his use of the F word. She'd never heard him curse at all. If anything, he seemed to go out of his way not to. Considering how many former military types she was around all the time she knew he was tempering his language around her. She liked the forceful way he denied wanting something casual, however. "Your sister Camilla told me you were dating somebody."

By his expression, it was clear she'd surprised him. Just as quickly his eyes narrowed. "Is that why you were being weird Monday night?"

"That's not an answer." And she found that she really, really needed one.

"*No.* I haven't dated anyone or looked at another woman since we met. I haven't wanted to. And...I don't think I'm going to want to look at another woman for a long time. As in, ever." There was a determined set to his jaw, and his expression when he looked at her was filled with a kind of raw hunger she'd never experienced from anyone.

Heat swept through her body like a wildfire, singeing all her nerve endings. She collapsed back against the passenger seat. Emerson wondered why his sister had lied to her but brushed that small hurt aside as she focused on the here and now and the fact that Carlito wanted her. From the sound of it, more than simply wanted to date. He wanted something serious and...so did she. It seemed too easy though, that this incredible man was just putting it all out there and admitting he wanted something real with her.

"I want Saturday to be a date too." Some days she could have pretended they actually were dating, for how much time they spent with each other. But she wanted the right to touch him, to kiss him, to see him completely naked and have her way with him, bringing him all sorts of pleasure... Her cheeks flushed at the thought, as she allowed herself to indulge in that fantasy without pulling back.

"I don't want to date anyone else, Emerson."

The way he said her name sent more delightful shivers down her spine. His tone was so serious, intent, she had no doubt he meant it. "Me neither." The second the words were out she knew she meant them too. She felt as if maybe they'd been building to this for a while and she'd been too blind to see it.

He took her hand as they reached the stoplight a corner away from their destination. When he linked his fingers through hers, it felt like the most natural thing in the world. Arousal punched through her as she imagined his hands gliding all over her naked body, teasing and caressing.

"I don't want to wait until Saturday night for a date." Tomorrow was Friday and if he wasn't working, she wanted to see him then too.

He smiled. "Good. I've already got reservations for us at Montez's Grill tomorrow night."

She blinked. It was one of her favorite restaurants. "What?"

"I came by your office tonight with the sole intent of asking you out, of making it crystal clear that I want more than friendship with you."

She'd completely forgotten to ask him why he'd stopped by the office tonight. Not that she was complaining. "It's...hot when you get all growly like that," she murmured, watching him closely. And she loved that he'd already made the reservations.

His wicked grin made her insides flip-flop again. Oh God, this man was going to wreak complete havoc on her system. She'd been fantasizing about what it would be like to be intimate with him, but it wasn't just a fantasy now. By all accounts, it was going to be a reality very soon. If she thought about it too much right now, however, she was going to combust.

She cleared her throat. "Why...do you think Camilla lied to me?" It hurt more than a little because they were friends. Or she thought they had been.

Carlito just shook his head. "I don't know why. But I can guarantee it wasn't to hurt you. She adores you, and has been after me to man up and ask you out forever. Her lying was probably some misguided attempt to..." He let out a short sigh that was more frustrated laugh than anything. "Honestly, who knows when it comes to my sisters or my mom? Sometimes I can't even try to understand their logic."

"So your family will be okay with us being together?" It wasn't a real fear—she adored his family—but she'd also just been his friend until now. Something else she was still trying to wrap her head around. If he wasn't dating anyone else and she wasn't... It felt weird to say the word *boyfriend* where Carlito was concerned, but that was essentially what he was now. Right? She wanted to crush her lips to his right freaking now and seal the deal, to get a taste of this man she considered hers.

"Oh yeah. They'll be more than happy. My mama's been after me to lock you down since the moment she met you."

Emerson flushed with pleasure at his words. His sisters and mom were important to him so it meant a lot that they approved of her. Not that she would have let that stop a relationship between her and Carlito if they didn't, but it made her incredibly happy. "I had no idea."

He pulled into a parking lot across the street from their destination, turned off the engine and twisted to face her. His fingers tightened around hers and yep, those little butterflies in her stomach took off again.

It was as if she'd been given a pure dose of adrenaline. Being around him, with him holding her hand so intimately and looking at her as if she were the most precious thing in the world, it was hard to keep a thought in her head.

"I kept putting off asking you out because I didn't want to ruin our friendship, but…I couldn't do it any longer. I want the right to hold your hand in public, to call you my own." He cupped the back of her head possessively. "To do this…" His voice was all growly again as he leaned forward.

Just as eager as him, she met him halfway.

The second their mouths met, all her nerve endings flared to life as if she'd been shocked. Energy rolled off him as he teased her mouth open, his kiss demanding and sensual. It was as if he invaded all of her, stripped all her barriers away with this one kiss. Moaning into his mouth, she clutched onto his shoulders as she nipped at his bottom lip. Right now was too much and not enough. And sweet Lord, if just a kiss was turning her into a puddle of sensation, she could only imagine how great it would be once they finally got naked.

When he pulled back, his eyes were full of tempered heat. "Let's go check on your friend." His voice was a soft growl.

A shiver streaked down her spine at the heat in his words. After they checked on Isa she planned to have some very private time with Carlito. Shelving that for now—and only because she absolutely had to—she nodded and fell into step with him. It was always quiet in the business district after dark. No restaurants or clubs were down here, and even though there were high-rise condos a few blocks over, there was no reason for people to be here. No, they'd go to areas like South Beach, Wynwood, Midtown, or even Brickell, which wasn't that far from here and had plenty of chic bars for the business crowd. It was always a little eerie when she left work late, and being near Raptor Aeronautical was no different.

"What are their security protocols?" Carlito asked as they crossed the four-lane road directly across from their destination.

Her hand fit perfectly in his and she savored the feel of holding his hand, his callused palm against hers. "About the same as Red Stone," Emerson said, looking up at the huge building looming in front of them. She frowned as she realized how dark the place was. Everywhere else was lit up sporadically, even though she knew most places were closed for the evening. Still, there should always be a couple lights on for late workers, the security team, and cleaning crews.

He nodded, as if he'd guessed that was the case. "I left my service weapon in the truck."

She lifted an eyebrow at him as they stepped up onto the sidewalk. "You still have another one on you though, don't you?"

He just gave her a sly grin. "If we have to go through security, then I'll bring it back out to my truck. But all we're planning to do is ask to page Isa, right?"

She nodded "Yes. And I really hope I'm just being stupid about all this."

"You're not being stupid." He tightened his fingers around hers as they neared the glass front door.

It was weird how natural it felt, after all this time of just being friends, moving into this new stage of their relationship. She really, really couldn't wait until they moved on to the next stage. He'd said he didn't want casual. And even though she told herself to slow down, she could see, well, everything with him. The whole deal. No white picket fence, because that wasn't her style, but...marriage, kids. *Yep.* She could see it all with Carlito. And it scared her only a little.

When he stopped about fifteen feet down the sidewalk from the main doors, she glanced at him. "What?"

He looked at the mostly dark building, then the neighboring buildings. "Maybe the reason she hasn't been able to call you is there's no power." His frown deepened even as she nodded. "I don't like the look of this." He pulled out his cell phone.

"What are you doing?"

"Gonna call one of my guys, see if there have been any power outage reports before we head in there blind." He didn't drop her hand as he typed in his security code.

"Okay." Fine by her.

He tugged her hand as he scrolled down to someone's name. "Come on, let's go back and wait in my truck."

They turned and Emerson froze at the same time Carlito stiffened, his phone up to his ear.

A man was pointing a gun directly at her face.

CHAPTER SIXTEEN

"Dammit." Graysen wanted to pound his fist against the desk, but took a deep breath instead.

"I haven't found anything either." Isa looked just as frustrated as he felt as she closed the last drawer of the filing cabinet she'd been searching.

They'd covered the entire office thoroughly trying to find the satellite phone—or any phone at this point.

"The last time I saw the satellite phone it was on his desk. The only thing I can think is that he put it in his safe." Which Graysen had found behind a painting. But he couldn't break into it.

"Can't you just open the safe?" Isa asked.

He arched an eyebrow. "Just because I used to work for the CIA doesn't mean I can break into heavily secured safes—not without the right tools, anyway."

"So what do you think we should do now?" Isa asked, frustration clear in her voice.

Before he could respond the radio attached to his belt made a slight static sound before a faintly accented voice came over the line. "If you can hear me, I know you are still here in the building. And we have two of your friends. A pretty blonde who I think could be very entertaining to my men. According to her ID her name is Emerson. If that means anything to you, meet me in the lobby in twenty minutes. I just want the information you have. Give it to me and your friends live."

"Oh my God, they have Emerson." Panic laced Isa's voice.

"Shit." Graysen scrubbed a hand over the back of his head. This changed everything.

"He said two of our friends. I can't imagine who else would be with her, other than maybe Harrison."

Graysen nodded. If Emerson had been worried about Isa, she'd have contacted their boss. "The only way I can see someone getting the drop on *him* is if maybe they had a weapon."

"Should we respond to them?"

"No. I don't want them to know we've received their message. The man might have just been fishing, trying to see if he could bait us into responding. Four of his men are dead so they've got to be getting nervous." And there was no way in hell he or Isa would survive if they went to the lobby.

"Maybe," she said, but didn't sound convinced. "That wasn't Alan Persky. I've talked to him enough the past week to know that."

"I agree." He'd talked to the man too. But even if it wasn't Persky, it didn't mean he wasn't working with whoever had just radioed them.

"What are we going to do? We've got to help her."

"I'm going to find and save Emerson." No way in hell she'd be in the lobby either.

She stepped around the desk, moved closer until inches separated them. "You can't go after her and whoever's with her by yourself. That's suicide."

"I've been up against worse odds." And he sure as hell wasn't leaving a vulnerable woman to fend for herself against armed men who'd threatened to make her their entertainment. There was no possible way he could do that and live with himself.

She blinked once before her lips pulled into a thin line. "Well you're not going alone. We'll figure something out together. And you can't go to the freaking lobby, it's a trap!"

He'd never admit it, but he liked her bossy tone—and the fact that she cared about his well-being. "I know it's going to be a trap. But that doesn't mean I can't go look for Emerson and whoever she's with," he said. He'd have to be a ghost, go floor by floor until he figured out where she was being held. It would take too much damn time, but there was nothing else to do since they hadn't found a sat phone and there was no damn Wi-Fi reachable from Hamilton's office to get a message out. No matter what, Isa wasn't going with him to find Emerson. It wasn't happening.

Isa shook her head. "No. I don't care how trained you are. You're one person against…who knows how many. There's got to be something else we can do."

"The best thing for *you* to do is to hide out in the private stairwell. Either that or directly here in the office, but I think the stairwell is the best place. There are only two entrances to it, so you'll know if someone is coming. And you'll be armed." He couldn't go after Emerson knowing that Isa would be in even more danger. Simply couldn't do it. And if she came with him, he'd be more worried about her than anything else. He couldn't have his attentions divided like that and be effective.

She just gritted her teeth and let out a frustrated sound. "If you're going to go after her, you're going to be prepared. I know how to make some quick and not-so-pretty smoke bombs. You can at least lay down some cover. You'll be blind going in once you discover where Emerson is, but the upside is that whoever these men are will be blind as well."

"You know how to make smoke bombs?" He did too. It was messy but he was fairly certain there were enough of the ingredients in the building to make them. And...it was a damn good idea.

She gave a harsh laugh. "My father actually taught me how to make them. Thought it was a useful skill to know. Among other things." There was a flash of bitterness in her eyes visible even under the muted lights from the city outside, but it faded quickly as she continued. "I think we can find enough of the supplies in Hamilton's private kitchen area, but if not we can find them in other kitchens or janitor closets. We can create enough havoc and distraction to really screw these guys up. If anything, maybe it will set off some alarm not connected to the power."

He nodded, liking this idea. "No matter what, it will create enough of a distraction, especially with the hallways already being darkened. But we're only doing it if the supplies are on this floor. I'm not putting you in any more danger looking for this stuff." If necessary, he'd do that on his own once he knew she was relatively safe.

"Fine." She might not like it, but Isa wasn't arguing with him, at least. Turning on her heel, she headed out of the office.

Her stiff body language made it clear she was annoyed with him.

"You'd rather I take you with me?" he asked as they reached the small kitchen. It wasn't happening.

There wasn't as much light in the smaller room, but there was enough streaming in from the oversized window that they could work.

Isa sighed, gave him an annoyed look. "No. I know I'll slow you down and...I'm definitely not trained enough to take on a bunch of armed guys. I just hate feeling useless."

Her honesty surprised him—and touched him. He liked that she was being real with him. "You're not useless."

She didn't respond as he opened the freezer, looked for cold packs because they contained ammonium nitrate. There were multiple ways to make smoke bombs and he was going for the fastest. If there weren't cold packs, he'd use another, dirtier way.

"I know a couple different ways to make these." Isa opened a cabinet, started pulling out sugar and paper towels.

"Me too. We'll probably have to use different methods to make as many as we can. And it's a good idea." A really good one. He'd simply planned to take out as many men as he could one-on-one with head or body shots, or in hand-to-hand combat, and keep looking for cell phones. Sometimes simplest was best, but using smoke bombs was unexpected and would definitely confuse his targets.

"Thanks. Never thought I'd get to use this particular knowledge."

They worked quickly together, making two different types of crude smoke bombs that would be effective. It took longer than he'd have liked, especially knowing Emerson was at the mercy of those men. If that bastard who'd radioed them really did start hurting Emerson after twenty minutes, Graysen was going to make him pay.

He just hoped she could hold on a little longer. Because he was damn sure going to find her.

* * *

"How did you get rid of your badge?" Emerson whispered to Carlito.

He shifted his feet slightly. Only a couple feet separated them in the darkness. They'd been zip-tied to shelves in a supply closet by armed men a few minutes ago. A single battery-powered lantern-style light sat on one of the shelves, casting shadows over her face, her stress clear. More than anything, Carlito wanted to reach out, comfort her—and get her the hell out of here.

He'd seen some tattoos on a couple of the men he guessed were Russian, but he didn't recognize them as gang tats. At least not local gangs.

"Sleight of hand." It had been a risk, but Carlito had tossed his badge and ID right before they'd been shoved through one of the main doors into the building. He was still pissed at himself for letting some asshole get the drop on him. That guy had come out of nowhere, but he should have been more aware. "For now, if they ask, my name is Carlito and I'm a new hire at Red Stone Security. You don't know me well, but asked me to come with you tonight." He knew enough about Red Stone because of Grant that he could bullshit if he needed to. And since he and Emerson weren't dead yet, he figured their captors might need them alive for something. Otherwise they would have just shot them once they'd gotten them into the privacy of the building. Keeping her alive and getting her the hell out of here was his only priority at the moment.

Before he could say anything else, one of the armed men opened the door and stepped inside the dim room. Carlito had overheard someone refer to the man as Dmitri. The man shut the door behind him and leaned against it, crossing his arms over his chest as he stared at the two of them.

"Why did you have a gun on you?" he asked Carlito.

Carlito kept his gaze steady. They'd found his pistol in his ankle holster almost immediately. "I'm in the security business. I always have one on me."

He turned his attention to Emerson. "Why are you here?"

Carlito answered even though the man wasn't looking at him. He wanted to keep all of the man's attention on him and not her. "We just stopped by to check on a friend who works here." It was a stupid answer, but what else was he going to tell the guy? So far these guys had no idea he was a cop, and he planned to keep it that way. He needed to keep things as vague as possible.

The man's eyes narrowed on Carlito. "Don't lie to me or I will start cutting her." To underscore his words, he withdrew a five-inch blade from a sheath. He held it at his side, clearly comfortable with a knife in his hand.

Carlito's blood chilled, but before he could respond, Emerson spoke up. "We're here because one of my coworkers called me. She was supposed to meet me and never showed up. That's it."

"Is this coworker named Isa?"

Emerson didn't respond but her expression gave her away.

The man looked at her thoughtfully for a long moment. "I radioed her, giving her time to meet me. I told her that if she doesn't show up, you're going to be entertainment for my men." The dark look in his eyes made Carlito go still.

The threat was undeniably true. Though he wanted to yank against his bonds, to kill this man for the threat he'd just made against the woman Carlito loved, he contained his rage. For now.

The man's hand-held radio squawked. The words were in Russian, but the tone was clear enough: there was a problem.

Without another word, Dmitri pulled out his radio and stepped out of the closet.

Emerson let out a small sound of distress, the fear on her face cutting at his insides.

"We're going to get out of this," Carlito whispered. He was going to do everything possible to get Emerson out of here. Or die trying. Because no one was hurting her.

Emerson jerked at her zip-tied hands. "How?"

There was no guarantee that once they got out of their bonds they would be able to escape. Not with armed men outside the door. But they had to take the chance.

He stood up straighter. "Tighten the zip ties like this." Using his teeth, he yanked on the tail of the tie. It started to cut off his circulation, but it was necessary for what he had to do.

"*Tighten* it?" she whispered.

He nodded. After she'd done it, he held his hands up slightly and eased his body back, keeping his hands stretched out in front of him. "Stand with your feet shoulder-width apart, like this."

She mirrored his action.

Under other circumstances, he would have slammed the heel of his palms against his pelvic bone, in an effort to snap the zip ties free. But with the metal pole in the way they were too constrained. Still, he was going to try the same tactic he knew worked, and slam his palms against the shelf instead.

A single shout of alarm came from the hallway, making him pause. When he didn't hear anything else, he ignored it. "Do exactly what I do."

Putting force behind the move, he jumped up slightly and slammed his hands down against where the shelf and pole were connected. The thud was loud but the ties snapped free. His palms and wrists ached but he ignored the pain. They had to free themselves fast before Dmitri or one of his men came back.

Emerson did the same but it didn't work.

"Keep trying," he whispered as he began searching for something to cut her free, and for weapons. He let out a growl of frustration when he found nothing but a couple mops. It would have to do for now. And it was better than nothing.

Snap.

He turned in time to find her broken ties falling to the ground. "Are you okay?"

She nodded, rubbing her wrists.

He held out a mop to her. "It isn't much, but you can shove the end into someone's throat or eye—anywhere that will do damage."

She nodded, her eyes widening as she pointed behind him. Thick white smoke was billowing under the doorway.

Fire.

Shit. "Stay close." Heart racing, Carlito eased the door open and peered out into the hallway. Or tried to.

A wall of smoke greeted him but…it didn't have the smell of a fire. It was an acrid stench, one he recognized from his PD training and the Corps. Listening, he didn't hear shouts of alarm either, which was…odd. He'd heard one person cry out earlier, but it had been quiet since then.

Maybe it was Graysen and Isa who'd created the smoke. And the guys who'd taken over this building were obviously professional enough not to shout and act like maniacs so, okay, not odd at all. No, they'd be stealthy as they tried to find the threat—which had to be Graysen.

This was their chance to escape. Would probably be their only one.

Carlito shut the door and scanned the shelves again, using the lantern to search. He reached for a box of cleaning supplies at the same time Emerson did. They both pulled out thin surgical-style masks the cleaning staff must use, and put them on.

"Hold on to the back of my pants. We'll use the darkness and smoke as cover. I'm going to stay close to the wall. If we're stopped, keep going and get somewhere safe. Do not stop for me." He kept his voice whisper quiet, but he knew she heard him.

She nodded but the look in her eyes said she wouldn't leave him.

No time to argue. Turning, he eased the door open again.

The dark-haired man with visible tattoos on his neck who'd originally pulled the gun on them stood there, clearly about to open the door. Surprise flashed over his face.

Carlito struck out, slamming his fist into the guy's throat. The Russian's whole body jerked back, his eyes widening. Before the man could react, Carlito punched him again, breaking his trachea. Then he grabbed him by the shoulders and head-butted him in the face.

As the guy crumpled under the assault, Carlito tugged him back into supply room, tossed him to the ground and stripped him of his hand-held radio and two weapons: a Glock—with a suppressor—and a knife. The guy wasn't dead, but he wouldn't be getting up anytime soon, and now Carlito had something to even the odds.

Emerson didn't make a sound, just stepped over the guy's body as Carlito opened the door again. It was difficult to see through the smoke. Only muted light from office windows created a sliver of illumination.

Staying close to the wall, he began creeping eastward, weapon at the ready. When they'd been brought to the third floor he'd paid attention to the nearest exits, and right now he and Emerson were about three doors down from the nearest stairwell. It was time to get the hell out of here and find somewhere to hole up.

He didn't think exiting through the lobby was an option and he didn't know this building well enough to make any tactical decisions. So his first mission was to get Emerson to safety. They could hunker down in an office far away from here. From there, they'd figure out what to do next.

CHAPTER SEVENTEEN

"What the hell is going on?" Alan demanded of one of the only two men currently in the lobby. Dmitri had taken the blonde woman and her security guy up to the third floor to question them a few minutes ago.

Dmitri had wanted to find out if anyone else knew why they'd come here—but something had happened. He'd heard Dmitri speaking rapid-fire Russian over the radio to one of the men in the lobby, and now Dmitri wasn't answering his calls.

"We're not sure." The man's voice was clipped. "There's some sort of smoke on multiple floors, but it's not a fire. Likely smoke bombs."

Smoke bombs? *Shit, shit, shit.*

This was getting way too out of hand. Hell, it had gotten out of hand hours ago. Too many people were dead and now there was no controlling the fallout. The man with Isa, Graysen whoever, had to be behind this. Unless the dark-haired bitch was doing it. He had a hard time imagining the delicate-looking woman killing Yuri's men and setting off smoke bombs, however.

But what the hell did he know? Considering who her father was, per Yuri's file, maybe she had lethal skills and she was the one behind all this havoc.

This was supposed to have been a way for him to cash out, start over somewhere new without anything hanging over his head. No ex-wife or alimony and no debt.

He was still going to split the country with Katya. But instead of coming in tomorrow then waiting it out a couple weeks like everything was normal, he was going to leave tonight. He'd tried calling his fiancée a couple times but she hadn't responded. That was making him more antsy as well. She always answered his calls or at least called him back in ten minutes.

He wouldn't have as much money as he'd have liked, but he could still start over in a Third World country and live like a king. Faking his own death should be easy enough. And he was certain that Hamilton had cash in the safe in his office. That should appease Katya enough.

Alan wasn't in the CEO's office much, but he had a key to get inside and he knew the combination to the safe. He'd take what was in there and leave.

As the armed Russian started talking into the radio again, Alan headed toward one of the exits. His heart raced out of control as the gravity of what he was doing settled in. Screw all this, he was done.

"Where are you going?" the man's voice called out across the lobby, the sound echoing.

He glanced over his shoulder but didn't bother slowing. "I don't answer to you." He shoved at the release bar, exiting into an enclosed hallway that led to one of the parking garages. From there he'd have to cross over to another parking garage and head up to Hamilton's office through the private stairwell.

Alan sneered at that. Hamilton was all about his privacy, didn't even let him use that exit. As if he didn't work just as hard as that bastard.

In the garage he immediately spotted two armed men, nodded at both of them and acted as if he had every damn right in the world to be doing what he was.

If he moved with purpose, it would look as if he was right where he was supposed to be. Out of the corner of his eye, he noted that neither of them got on their radios to let Dmitri know what he was doing.

Good.

He turned his own radio on as he breached the entrance with his key. He heard Dmitri talking on it in quiet tones, in Russian, and tuned the man out. Then Alan turned on his flashlight since the dim orange glow from the generator didn't provide enough light for him.

Gritting his teeth, he started jogging up the stairs, ignoring the ache in his chest as he kept pushing forward. He was more out of shape than he'd realized. It took a while to reach Hamilton's office because of all the stairs.

Breathing hard, he stopped only when he was at the top. He bent over at the waist, sucked in air.

Move, move, move, he ordered himself. He'd berate himself later for being out of shape. When he tried the door, he stilled when he found it unlocked.

Pulling out a gun Dmitri had given him, he slowly opened the door. There were no signs of life in the wide-open assistant's area. Still, he stepped out carefully. Sweat rolled down his spine as he listened.

Fear and exertion pressed in on him. His heart was pounding too hard for him to hear much but he took a few more steps toward the assistant's desk, scanning everywhere as he moved.

There were a lot of windows on the top floor and light from the city streamed in, giving more than enough illumination to see where he was going. No smoke up here, so that was something.

He doubted Isa or her partner had made it all the way up here.

"Drop your gun or I shoot," a quiet female voice said from his right.

Out of the corner of his eye he saw Isa step out of the kitchen area, a gun in her hand, pointing it directly at him.

He could try to swivel and shoot her, but...he wasn't sure if she was a good shot or not. Considering who her father had been and the fact that four of Dmitri's men were dead... Yeah, he couldn't take the chance that she was the lethal killer who'd taken out men who were supposed to be the best.

He stayed still, watching her every move. It would be better to wait until he was closer to her, try to overpower her. If he tried now he'd just end up getting shot.

"I'm putting it down now." His voice shook as he slowly bent, set it on the floor.

"Turn slowly and kick it over to me." Her voice was deadly calm.

Ice slithered along his veins, but he did as she said. He was afraid not to. If the bitch gave him an opening, he was going to take it. No way was he getting brought down by some woman.

***

Graysen plastered himself against the wall of one of the offices. The smoke on this floor was starting to thin out and he had only two smoke bombs left. He'd used most of them on floors two through seven, trying to weed out where Emerson was being held. It wasn't the best plan, but he'd been hoping they'd move the prisoners if he smoked them out.

He listened to the low crackle static of a hand-held radio from the only man he'd seen on this floor so far.

A man's voice came over it in Russian, stating in frustrated terms that the two prisoners had escaped. Graysen understood him perfectly.

Yes! Relief punched through him that Emerson was free. He hadn't known her long but she was sweet and innocent. The thought of her at the mercy of these men made him see red.

Waiting another moment, he listened as the man responded in quiet tones. It sounded as if they were running low on men, and the plan was to hunt down the blonde and her security partner. So it must be somebody who worked for Red Stone. Not that it really mattered who was with Emerson, as long as they were capable and kept her safe. Graysen felt better knowing she'd escaped, even if he had no idea where to start searching for her.

Now that he knew she was unharmed, he needed to head back up to Isa. They'd been separated for too long, and he couldn't stand being away from her like this. No matter how safe she might be up in Hamilton's office.

And right now safe was a very relative term. Until they were out of this building and these men were either under arrest or dead, he wouldn't rest.

Soft footfalls sounded in the hallway, leading away from him. Graysen slowly peered out of the office door. The smoke was more of a haze now. He could only see one man in the hallway.

Weapon in hand he stepped out, ready to take down the guy, when the man swiveled. Moving lightning fast, the man dove through an open door up ahead.

Thud. Thud.

Bullets slammed through the wall next to the doorway the man had jumped through, hitting the wall closest to Graysen's head. Graysen crouched and returned fire. He could run or try to finish the guy.

He wasn't the running type.

He heard a soft thud and a cry of pain, but the man could be faking. He continued firing until he emptied his weapon. Then he withdrew his backup weapon.

Thud. Thud. Thud.

Three more bullets slammed into a door across the hall and a few feet away from Graysen. The guy's aim was way off so maybe Graysen had hit him.

Heart racing, he eased back a few steps and slipped into the nearest doorway. For all he knew this guy was calling for backup. In fact, he had to be, unless he was completely stupid. Graysen couldn't hear the guy calling on the radio but these guys could have phones. So far he hadn't found any on the men he'd killed, but no way in hell was he going to get trapped down here.

Keeping his weapon trained on the far doorway, he eased out again, giving up cover as he hurried back down the hall and away from the shooter. He needed to put distance between this floor and himself as soon as possible.

As he neared the end of the hall, only feet from the stairwell door, it flew open.

Graysen barely had time to react.

Turning, he aimed and fired. Crimson bloomed between the man's eyes before he fell to his knees. Before the body hit the floor, Graysen swiveled, knowing he would be attacked from behind. The man who had fired on him before was in the hallway, staggering. He raised his weapon with one hand, his other hanging limply at his side.

Graysen aimed, fired. The man swayed suddenly and Graysen only grazed his face.

Thud. Thud. Thud.

Bullets embedded in the ceiling, wall and floor as the man fell to the ground, his arm flailing wildly as he stumbled.

Graysen pulled the trigger again. This time his aim was true. Another head shot.

The man's body dropped. Graysen didn't bother watching him hit the ground, just turned and hurried through the open stairwell door. Carefully and quietly, he let it close behind him.

He listened, heard footsteps somewhere above him, and he eased back out into the hallway. There was no movement, so he sprinted back down it, looking for another stairwell entrance. He'd killed eight men by this point.

He wasn't certain how many more were here, but eight meant he'd hurt the crew here. They had to be getting angry, and when people were angry they did stupid things, acted rashly.

He just hoped that by thinning out these killers, it would help them escape more easily. Because he and Isa were getting the hell out of this building sooner rather than later.

It took him another ten minutes to make it back to the top floor because he had to move slowly. He agonized every second he was away from Isa. Not being able to contact her, not knowing if she was okay—it carved him up inside.

As he entered the lobby outside Hamilton's office, he froze when he heard a male voice.

"I can help you get out of here." It sounded like Persky.

Rage filled Graysen at the sound of the man who was responsible for putting Isa in danger. Moving quietly, he hurried toward the open doorway of Hamilton's office.

Weapon up, he couldn't hide his shock when he saw Persky plastered against the huge window overlooking the city. The man's hands were above his head and firmly against the window as he faced the cityscape.

And Isa was holding him at gunpoint.

She pushed out a sigh of relief when she saw Graysen standing there. "I didn't want to get too close to him. So I made him stand like that so I could see his every move."

Smart. He couldn't believe how steady she was. "Did he hurt you?"

"No. He never touched me. I got the drop on him." Her voice was filled with just a hint of pride.

Graysen nodded in approval. Damn, she was something. "Don't take your weapon off him."

"No problem."

Keeping an eye on Persky by the window, Graysen found a tie in the personal armoire Hamilton had filled with extra suits. He wrenched Persky's arms behind his back and secured his wrists together, ignoring the grunt of pain the man made.

"Watch the door," he said softly to Isa, who nodded. He returned his attention to the bastard who was behind all this. "How many of your guys are in the building?"

"Fuck you," Persky snarled.

Graysen grabbed the back of Persky's head, twisting his fingers in the man's hair. Then he slammed his face into the window. The sickening crunch of his nose breaking sounded in time with the window rattling ominously.

The man cried out in pain. "Twelve, twelve!"

Graysen shoved Persky's face against the window, ignoring his continuing cries of agony "Twelve exactly?"

Persky's face was scrunched up in pain, but he shook his head. "Fourteen total. Including me."

Graysen had taken out eight men so five were left, since he had Persky. He really, really liked those odds. He could take out five more guys, no problem.

That was, if Persky was actually telling the truth. Since he didn't have time to question the guy and gauge if he actually was, Graysen was still going to be cautious. He patted Persky down, searching for weapons or a phone. Found nothing. Of course not. Why would life be that damn easy? "Where's your phone?"

"In the lobby," he rasped out, blood trailing over his lips.

"Why don't you have it?"

"Left it in case…they tried to track me."

Well wasn't that interesting. Maybe Persky was bailing on his partners. Graysen didn't care at this point. He just wanted to get the hell out of here with Isa. He wanted to know, in very specific detail, why the hell Persky and his men had attacked this place, but wouldn't waste time questioning him now. They'd get their answers later.

He grabbed Persky's bound wrists, turned and shoved him toward the exit. Graysen looked at Isa. "If this bastard is telling the truth, there are only five guys left. I've already taken out eight. We'll go down through the private stairwell." He yanked Persky to a sudden stop. "How many men are in the parking garage?"

"Only…o…one that I saw." The man was trembling now, the stench of fear rolling off him palpable.

Graysen couldn't afford to believe him. "Stay behind me," he murmured to Isa, who still had her weapon in hand.

She nodded, her expression tight, and quickly moved behind him as they headed for the stairwell. They'd hidden her laptop in Hamilton's office but he knew she still had the flash drive tucked into her skirt pocket. One way or another, this information was getting to the right people.

"How were you planning on getting out of here?" Graysen asked Persky.

He didn't answer right away so Graysen slammed his face against the wall by the stairwell exit door. The drywall cracked under the impact and when he pulled Persky back, a smear of blood stained the pale blue wall.

The man screamed in pain.

"Shut the fuck up." Rage pulsed through Graysen, the urge to kill this monster right here and now nearly overwhelming. "You put the woman I love in danger, sent men to kill her. I will start putting bullet holes in you if you don't answer me when I ask a question." His tone was calm, which he knew would terrify Persky more than if he'd yelled. *Good.* He wanted the man pissing-his-pants scared. Because Graysen meant every damn word. He didn't relish torturing people but he'd do whatever it took to get the truth from Persky.

He made a sniffling, gurgling sound and spit out blood onto the floor. "Company car...has keys in the console. Big, white Cadillac. Bullet...resistant." His words came out nasal-sounding.

"You planning on ditching your partners?"

Surprising Graysen, Persky nodded. "This wasn't supposed...to happen. Was supposed to be easy money." He sniffled again, his words almost slurred now.

"What about Raptor's security people?" Graysen already knew something must have happened to the security team unless the guys were in on whatever this thing was.

Persky swallowed hard. "Dead."

Graysen gritted his teeth as he rested his hand on the release bar. He wanted to pummel Persky again for the admission. Who knew how many security guys had been murdered because they'd had the bad luck to be on the wrong shift. He couldn't think about that now.

"You ready?" he murmured to Isa.

"Yeah."

Though he wanted to pull her into his arms, to comfort her somehow, he couldn't. He'd save it for later. For once they got out of here.

It seemed to take forever to get down the seventeen floors since Persky was having a hard time keeping pace. The man was out of shape, but Graysen had messed his nose up and his breath was sawing in and out as if he'd pass out at any moment. If Graysen had to guess, the guy was about to lose it completely. He must have had grand plans to try to rip off his company and now everything had gone to shit for him. If Graysen could just stash him somewhere he would, but he couldn't risk Persky getting free or warning someone that they were attempting an escape from the building. Plus he was making damn sure this guy was delivered to the cops.

At the bottom of the stairwell, he turned to Isa. "If shit goes sideways—"

"I'm not leaving you, so save it." Even in the muted orange light he could see her determined expression.

"You're so stubborn."

"Yeah, I am... Did you mean what you said up there, that you still love me?"

The words had just slipped out when he'd been threatening Persky. Because Persky *had* put the woman he loved in danger. He kept his gaze locked on her. "Yes." He turned away before she could respond because he didn't want to see pity in her eyes. He loved her. Had never stopped.

She might consider everything between them a lie, and he understood it. Didn't mean it had all been a lie to him.

"We're going to use the vehicles as cover to the main exit—which will be to the west. If you try to alert anyone, I'll put a bullet in your head. Got it?" he snarled to Persky, who just nodded.

Once they were out in the garage everything was a hell of a lot darker. And colder. He wished he'd found shoes for Isa, hated that her feet were all torn up. The socks he'd taken from one of the dead men would just have to do for now.

They were on the bottom floor at least and wouldn't have to hike up or down floors in the garage. The only problem was, the actual exit was guaranteed to be guarded.

It didn't sound as if it would be heavily watched, considering how many guys Graysen had taken down. But there was also the possibility that Persky was lying about how many people were here. Considering the guy had no moral code, Graysen was betting there were more armed men.

Icy wind cut through his shirt as he shoved Persky toward a four-door truck to their right. It wasn't the best cover but it would have to do. Once they were all behind it, he lifted his head, scanned the rest of this floor of the garage.

Streams of outside light, probably from a neighboring building, illuminated the exit about fifty yards away. Multiple rows of parking and concrete barriers were in their way—not to mention heavily armed men potentially lurking around.

He pointed to a car three spots away. It would be their next cover. Persky nodded as Isa did the same.

Graysen stepped out first, using Persky as a human shield and making sure Isa was directly behind him. His rubber-soled boots and the rustle of their clothing barely made a sound as they moved but all the hair on the back of his neck rose.

That intrinsic survival instinct kicked in just as a man holding a pistol stepped out from behind a van in the parking row across from them.

"Drop your weapon!" Graysen held his pistol out past Persky's body, but still held Persky close as a human shield and never took his eyes off his target. The man paused. "Get behind that car, Isa," he murmured, loud enough for only her to hear. "I need you safe so I can take care of this."

The car was parked right up against a wall so no one would be able to sneak up on her from behind, at least. Graysen angled his body, nudging Isa to move. He was aware of her doing so, but kept his attention solely on the blond-haired man with a weapon. No silencer on this one.

"You think I care about this sniveling piece of shit?" The man's accent was faint, as with the other men from the building, and it was definitely Russian. His gaze flicked to Isa briefly as she moved, but he didn't seem concerned with her as he looked back at Graysen.

Graysen couldn't hear anyone else converging on them, but that didn't mean they weren't around. *Hell.*

Graysen didn't recognize the man from earlier, but...he knew the face from somewhere. It took all of two seconds for it to sink in. He'd seen the man on multiple Most Wanted lists.

Yuri Mikhailov.

"I think you do, Yuri Mikhailov. Surprised you're in the country when you're wanted for so many crimes."

The man's head tilted slightly to the side. He was too far away for Graysen to know for certain if he'd surprised him, but that change in body language was a giveaway.

"You would be wrong. Persky here was trying to flee the country, weren't you?" Ice coated his words.

Persky didn't respond, just breathed harder in Graysen's hold.

Pop. Pop.

Graysen shoved Persky forward into the bullets' path, while firing in return. Yuri dove behind a nearby Jeep. Graysen did the same, throwing himself toward where Isa was hiding—as a searing, tearing pain ripped through his chest.

CHAPTER EIGHTEEN

Isa crouched down in front of Graysen as he struggled to sit up.

Oh God.

Blood covered his shirt, seemed to be spreading everywhere. He had on a vest, but it didn't cover everything. So much blood was coming from his shoulder area, spreading outward in a hideous circle.

She had pretty much zero medical knowledge but pressed a hand to his shoulder where most of the blood seemed to be coming from. "Were you hit more than once?"

Grimacing, he nodded and tried to sit up again.

"Stay put," she whispered.

She held her hand to his shoulder, trying to fight back her own panic. She'd seen him shoot at the man named Yuri after the guy had shot Persky—who was lying in a pool of his own blood about ten feet away. She assumed Persky was dead, but wasn't going to check his pulse to make sure.

"I'm okay. I'm okay," he murmured, his eyes starting to lose focus. "Gotta make sure he's down." He shoved her hand away with surprising force and managed to sit up fully.

She noticed that he held onto his side as he moved, winced. Panic punched through her when she saw more blood seeping through his fingers against his side.

"Yes, you're fine. You are going to be completely fine. You have to be. Because I still love you." Graysen didn't respond. His eyes drooped, his head falling back against the rear of the trunk.

Shit. Shit. Shit. This was not good. She had to get help, had to get a phone. She'd never realized how much she'd grown to depend on her cell phone. Now not having one, not being able to call for help at the touch of a button when the man she loved was wounded? It was terrifying.

She rolled onto her side and looked under the car. Her throat tightened. Two booted feet were slowly inching their way toward them from across the garage. She couldn't even hear the man's movements. She'd been so focused on Graysen, and stopping the flow of blood. She should have been paying better attention.

No way was this guy going to win, going to take away the man she still loved. They'd fought like hell to make it this far tonight. They were damn well going to escape.

Going on instinct, she grabbed her weapon from the ground and fired at the man's legs and ankles. She might not like using guns, but her father had made sure she knew how to use one.

His grunt of pain rent the air as he fell to the ground, landing with a thud. She had a perfect visual of him under the car. Yuri, the man who'd shot Graysen. He'd fallen on his side and was facing her. Ice cold blue eyes stared back at her, his expression murderous.

His gun was still in his hand. He swung it toward her, his jaw clenched tight.

Time seemed to stretch out as she rolled over onto her belly, fired again at his face.

She pulled the trigger over and over until her gun made a *clicking* sound.

Breathing hard, she stared at the bloody mess of the man's face before she shoved up from her position. Bile rose in her throat but she swallowed it down. She'd freak out later.

"He's down," she said, hunkering next to Graysen, whose eyes were now shut. "Please don't die," she whispered.

She needed to get his vest off, to stanch the bleeding better, but first she had to find a phone. Had to get help.

"I'm going to call for help. I...love you, Graysen. I love you so much. Please live for us. We deserve a second chance."

His eyes fluttered open but he didn't respond. Just stared at her with hazy, blue eyes. Okay, that was good. He was awake, even if he wasn't talking. But his breathing sounded bad and his face was gray.

"Just hang on," she whispered before peering around the car. Her heart pounded erratically in her chest. The man named Yuri was definitely dead. His face and head were pretty much gone. She forced the bile back. *Focus,* she ordered herself.

Just because he was dead didn't mean there weren't others hiding. Steeling herself, she picked up one of

Graysen's guns and pushed up slowly to her knees, then feet.

She couldn't see anyone in the darkened garage. Couldn't hear any footsteps. Couldn't hear...anything.

On silent, aching feet she crept toward Yuri's body. He was covered in blood, his face looking more like pulverized meat than human. Her stomach roiled again as she began patting him down.

She nearly cried out in relief when her blood-slicked fingers clasped a phone in his front pants pocket. With trembling fingers, she yanked it out. It had a security lock, of course. But she didn't need to get past that to call the police. She swiped the emergency call icon and made the call, but froze at a faint shuffling sound to her left.

Her throat clenched in horror as she made eye contact with a dark-haired man in tactical gear just like the other men she'd seen tonight.

He lifted a gun.

Her fingers clenched around her own gun but she knew it was too late. Grief speared her at the thought of dying without having another chance with Graysen, knowing that Graysen would now be at this man's mercy.

Puff. Puff.

She jerked, expecting pain as bullets tore through her—but the armed man fell to his knees instead, eyes frozen wide as blood bloomed across his forehead.

She swiveled to see Graysen crouched on his knees behind her, gun in hand, face pale. The weapon clattered to the concrete right before he collapsed.

"9-1-1 operator, how may I assist you?" The sound of the emergency operator's voice on the other end of the phone made her cry out with relief.

Her entire body shook as she answered. "There's been an attack at Raptor Aeronautical. My friend has been shot. We're in the parking garage and need help now! There might be other armed men here! They've killed a lot of people." She shoved up and hurried back to Graysen. She put the phone on speaker as she skidded to a halt in front of him.

His face was ashen, his breathing harsh and his head lolling to the side. More blood pooled around his torso, glistening darkly in the muted light coming in from outside. At least he was breathing.

She fell to her knees beside him and ripped off the vest before pressing her hands to the wound. Tears gathered in her eyes and a burning lump formed in her throat.

Don't die. You can't die on me. Not now.

He had to make it. She refused to believe they'd come this far only to lose him when she'd finally realized she still loved him.

* * *

Emerson jumped next to Carlito as lights suddenly flooded the small utility closet they were hiding in. He held a finger to his mouth, in case she was going to speak. He didn't think she would, but he wanted to be careful. With the lights now back on, they should be able to make a phone call from one of the landlines. But he wasn't sure if this was some sort of trick from the terrorists or whoever these guys were.

He started to motion that he was going to step outside and find a phone to call for help, when a familiar voice came over a central com system.

"Emerson, this is Harrison. I'm with the police right now. We're in the building. Isa and Graysen are on their way to the hospital. We are currently searching the building. Do not come out if you are hiding somewhere. We will find you. If you have access to a phone, call me to confirm. But if you're hiding and safe, stay where you are."

Hell, yeah. Carlito pulled Emerson into his arms, buried his face against her neck as she tightened her grip around him.

"Thank God. Everything is going to be okay." Her voice trembled a little.

Carlito held on tight, knew without a doubt that he was never letting this woman go. He'd known for a while that she was it for him, but tonight had confirmed it. He didn't want to live in a world without Emerson in it.

It couldn't be good that Isa and Graysen were going to the hospital, but he'd worry about that later. He was just thankful this nightmare was over.

Still holding her, he pulled back so he could look at her face. "You're coming to my house tonight. Just so there is no misunderstanding about how tonight will go. I'm not letting you out of my sight, probably for the next couple weeks. So you're just going to have to deal with the fact that you'll be moving into my place. I could lie and say it'll be temporary but...once I've got you under my roof, I'm not letting you go. You're mine and no one's taking you away from me."

Emerson gave him the widest smile, easing the worry that she might argue with him. "I really like this bossy, possessive side of you," she murmured.

"It's always been there, at least where you are concerned. You bring it out in me." And he wasn't going to fight it. She was his, simple as that.

CHAPTER NINETEEN

Graysen struggled to open his eyes. He needed to get to Isa. Needed to stop the shooter...

Beep. Beep. Beep.

He blinked, saw that he was in a bed and Isa was in a chair next to it—holding his hand. She was slouched down on the chair, eyes closed, her head tipped slightly back against a pillow tucked between the chair and her head. She had on a pair of jeans and a long-sleeved black sweater.

"Isa—" The word came out raspy, barely audible. He needed water.

Her eyes flew open. She blinked a few times as she pushed up in the seat. Relief filled her expression as her gaze locked with his. "Thank God you're awake. I'll get the nurse." She jumped up from her seat.

"Water," he rasped out. He didn't want a nurse, he just wanted Isa.

She froze two steps from the bed, nodded and poured water from the beige-colored pitcher on a table in the corner into a plastic cup of the same bland color. Some sloshed over the side in her haste but she hurried back to him and held it up to his lips.

He tried to raise his right hand to take it, realized he couldn't. It was in a sling. He lifted his left hand but ended up letting her tilt the cup for him. The cool, fresh liquid was heaven. After he drank it down in two gulps, she refilled the cup again.

This time he took it, and drank three more cups until he felt somewhat sated. "What...happened after I shot that guy? How are your feet?" They'd been so torn up from her running around without shoes.

She blinked once before setting the pitcher back down. "My feet are fine." Her expression softened as she took his hand between hers. "I should be asking you how you're feeling."

He rolled his left shoulder once. He felt as if he was in a haze, probably from whatever meds he was on. "Good... What happened? Is Emerson—"

"She's okay. She's actually here right now, in the waiting room. I sent her home last night but she's back. There's a lot to explain but right now you don't need to worry about it. You don't need to worry about anything. You saved me from that shooter and then Harrison and the cops came in and took over." She lifted his hand to her lips, kissed it briefly as she closed her eyes. "I almost lost you." Pain reverberated in her words.

His fingers tightened around hers, his heart squeezing. "I'm here and you're here." And...he remembered pain. "Was I shot more than once?"

She opened her eyes at his question, nodded. "Twice. In the shoulder and ribs."

He nearly snorted, but didn't want to cause himself any more pain. That was the problem with tactical vests. They covered a lot, but not nearly enough.

"You lost a lot of blood, but the doctors say you're going to be okay. They'll be able to tell you all the specific medical jargon I barely understand, but the important thing is no organs were hit and you've pulled through the worst. And the man who shot you is dead."

He remembered that, even with the haze of the meds making his brain fuzzy. "You killed him."

Her face tightened. "Yeah."

"Did I imagine… Did you tell me you loved me?" God, he hoped it hadn't been a hallucination. Those words were etched into his brain. He prayed that wasn't just his imagination. Her words were crystal clear in his head when everything else was fuzzy. *Please don't die. I'm going to call for help. I…love you, Graysen. I love you so much. Please live for us. We deserve a second chance.*

"I did."

"Did you mean it?" He needed to know right now. If she'd just said it in the heat of the moment, he needed to know.

She cupped his cheek, her expression soft. "Graysen—"

A doctor strode in then, a compact woman with caramel-colored skin and ink-black hair. She gave him a quick smile. "Glad to see you're awake. I'm Doctor Garcia, head of trauma surgery. Do you remember me?"

He strained, vaguely remembered being in an ambulance, Isa shouting at him to stay alive. He thought Harrison might have been at the hospital too. But he didn't remember this woman. And he hated that he couldn't remember her if he was supposed to. For a former CIA operative, having blackouts in his memory made him edgy. "No," he gritted out.

"That's normal for what you've been through. Your shoulder was grazed and your ribs were hit. Not broken, though. Your lung collapsed under the impact but it wasn't actually hit. Which is *really* good. But you're going to be sore for a few weeks. After two surgeries we got you stabilized and you're in recovery. I'm going to have you start on deep breathing and coughing exercises to minimize the chance of you getting pneumonia, but things are looking really good."

He listened as she went over how long it would take him to recover and how lucky he'd been, but most of his focus was on Isa, who'd moved to one of the windows. It was late afternoon, considering the angle of the sun, and he wondered what day it was if he'd had multiple surgeries. He also wanted an answer to his earlier question. Right now he didn't give a shit what the doctor had to say. He was alive and fine. He wanted to know how Isa felt about him. Whether they still had a chance.

"The police would like to speak to you, but I've let them know that's only happening if you're up to it." The doctor's words made him tear his gaze away from Isa.

"Yeah, I'm fine." He wanted some answers, anyway.

"I'm going to get Carlito," Isa murmured, hurrying out the door before he could stop her.

"Your fiancée has been a rock. She hasn't left the entire time you've been here," Dr. Garcia said to him.

He nearly jolted at the word fiancée, but kept his reaction to himself. If Isa wanted to say she was engaged to him, he was more than okay with that. He wanted her to wear his ring, for the entire world to know she was his. But was she? Was that what she wanted?

The doctor squeezed his hand once before turning at the sound of the door opening.

Carlito Duarte, a detective with the Miami PD walked in—Graysen recognized him because he was friends with Grant Caldwell, but mainly because he'd seen the guy at Red Stone multiple times.

"Hey, Mariana." The detective smiled warmly at the doctor.

"Detective. I'm only allowing this because he's awake and says he's okay—and I trust you. If his condition changes, one of you page me," she said, looking back at Graysen. "Got it? You might be out of the worst of it, but you need a lot of sleep right now."

"I'll let him know if I need a break," he said, when all he wanted to know was where Isa had gone.

She nodded. "Good. Your morphine will be kicking in again soon anyway."

"Mr. West," the detective began as the doctor left. He pulled up a chair next to his bed, his expression serious. "I know we've met, but officially, I'm Detective Duarte. Carlito, if you'd prefer. I'm sorry to do this now but I want to get your statement on the record. Technically I can't tell you this, but I'm doing it anyway. I can pretty much guarantee the State's Attorney won't be bringing charges against you. You're not under arrest, nor does the Miami PD plan to arrest you. If anything, they might give you a medal."

"Okay." He'd known there would be an inquiry after he'd killed so many men. Yes, it had been in self-defense, but that was a hell of a lot of bodies to deal with. Not to mention all the other bodies he hadn't been responsible for. Talk about a clusterfuck.

"I just need to get the facts on the record so we can match up everyone's timelines."

That was fair enough. "Isa said Emerson was okay." He took a shallow breath, struggled against his throbbing shoulder and chest. While he didn't doubt Isa, Graysen was still worried something might have happened to Emerson while she'd been captive. "How'd she fare?"

The man's expression softened. "She's good. Out in the waiting room with Isa right now. I was there Thursday, trapped with her."

He blinked, surprised. "Glad she had you with her."

"I know you came for her, so before I start taking notes I just want to say thank you." Expression serious, Carlito held out a hand.

Graysen took it and nodded. He'd have searched for anyone on his team, but it was clear Emerson meant something to the detective.

Shifting slightly against the starchy sheets, he tried to get comfortable. "What day is it?"

"Saturday."

Okay, so he'd only lost a day and change in his memory. He could deal with that. He leaned back as Carlito started in with the questions.

They were expected, if monotonous, but all he wanted to do was see Isa. Hold her, touch her, remind himself she was real and okay. That they were both alive and not stuck in that building. He also had a ton more questions about what had gone down, but knew the detective wouldn't be answering them. He'd have to get his answers from Harrison and Isa.

Then he wanted to know when they could get the hell out of the hospital and he could finally be alone with her.

* * *

Isa stood next to one of the windows in the small waiting room, resisting the urge to pace. She knew Graysen was just answering questions, but she wanted to be with him. Unfortunately, they were already bending the rules by allowing Carlito to question him instead of the lead detective assigned to the case. Harrison had asked for a favor and received it—no surprise.

Graysen—meaning, Red Stone Security—had stopped terrorists on US soil. Right now, the city was grateful, even as the media was going batshit crazy over what had happened. She didn't think they'd ever know the real story, the real reason those men had been at Raptor Aeronautical. And she didn't care.

The only thing that mattered was that Graysen, Emerson, Carlito, and she were okay. She hated that other innocents hadn't been so lucky.

"You want some tea or coffee?" Mara asked from her seat a few feet away. Wearing dark pants, knee-high boots and a cashmere sweater, she looked incredible as always.

"I'm okay, but thanks." Now that Graysen was awake she felt as if she could breathe normally again, but her nerves were still in tatters. She was sure he had a ton of questions and she wanted to answer all of them, especially if they were about *them*. But mainly, she just wanted to see him before he fell asleep again. "How's Belle?" she asked in an effort to talk about anything else.

Mara gave her a serene smile. "Fine. Just like she was the last time you asked an hour ago."

"Gah, sorry." She knew Belle was more than fine. She'd gone into labor Thursday night at a family dinner. Everyone had rushed to the hospital, some forgetting their cell phones and others ignoring calls. There had been complications with the birth and Belle had ended up having an emergency C-section. Which was why they hadn't been able to get hold of anyone when they needed to during the hostage situation. It had been a perfect storm of insanity. "You can go see her if you want. Don't feel like you've got to stick around here." She leaned against the window, trying to tamp down her rampant nerves.

"Trust me, I think she's had enough of family for a while. Last I heard, she and Grant were holed up in her room and not letting anyone else in. I think they needed some alone time with the baby before they leave this evening. My sweet little niece." Mara's expression softened so much it was strange to see.

Isa adored Mara, but the former operative wasn't a mushy or emotional woman. "You getting baby fever?" she asked.

Mara just snorted, shook her head. "Babies are fun to play with, then send home."

Harrison strode in carrying a tray of cups. "Amen to that. I think my brothers have lost their minds when it comes to their kids... Hey Isa, got you a hot chocolate. You need something warm right now. How's our man?"

"He's decent, I think. His color was better and he's talking to Carlito now."

Harrison gave a brisk nod. "Good. I want to see him before he falls asleep again." Guilt flickered in his dark eyes as he focused on her. It disappeared quickly, but she knew it had been there. He seemed to feel responsible for them not being able to get hold of him when they'd needed to. Well, no one could have predicted the shit that went down Thursday night and into Friday morning, so she certainly wasn't angry at him.

Even though she hadn't thought she wanted anything to drink, she gratefully took the cup. It warmed her fingers, taking off some of the edge. She wouldn't feel settled until Graysen was officially discharged from the hospital.

"Where's Emerson?" she asked after taking that first hot sip.

Harrison tilted his chin toward the direction of the exit. "In the cafeteria, grabbing some food. She said she'd be back soon, that she wanted to see Graysen now that he's awake."

Isa nodded, glad Emerson would be coming back. As far as Isa knew, Emerson had gone to the police station to answer questions, then home to change, and then come straight to the hospital. Mara had brought Isa clothes, and she'd showered in an empty room because she hadn't been about to leave the hospital.

It felt like forever, but was probably only twenty minutes before Carlito returned. The detective immediately went to the side of Emerson, who'd only arrived five minutes before, and wrapped his arm around her shoulders. It was clear to anyone watching, the man was smitten. And vice versa; Emerson looked at him as if he hung the moon.

He faced the group with a tired half-smile. "He's still awake, but looking pretty exhausted. Everything he said lines up with your timeline and ours," he said to Isa before looking at the others. "He wants to see everyone, but especially you, Isa. I'm gonna hang back, give you guys some space."

"Me too." Mara nodded. "You three go see him."

"Thanks." Isa was beyond ready to get back to Graysen. She'd been here since he'd been brought in, had refused to let the paramedics look at her feet until they'd gotten him into surgery. She had a few cuts and bruises. So freaking what? He'd been *shot*. If it hadn't been for the vest, he might have died right in front of her.

Something she didn't want to think about.

Isa didn't think Graysen was supposed to have more than one or two visitors at a time, but no one stopped them as the three of them made their way to his room. Maybe Harrison or Carlito had said something to the staff—or maybe Harrison had called in one of his favors. The man seemed to know everyone in the city.

Her heart rate kicked up as she pushed the door to Graysen's room open. She hated being away from him, even for twenty minutes. His face lit up when he saw her. The sight was a punch of awareness to all of her senses. She wasn't sure how she'd thought she could have ever lived without this man. Then to almost lose him—it was simply too much.

She headed straight for his bedside. She'd already told the staff that he was her fiancé so she would be allowed access to his room. And Harrison certainly hadn't corrected the staff.

Graysen took her hand as soon as she reached for him, linking his fingers through hers in a solid grip. Another healthy dose of relief slid through her at his firm hold.

"How are you feeling?" she asked, watching his face for exhaustion. He was the type of man to push himself too hard. Right about now, she wished they were alone so she could tell him how much she loved him, that she wanted to start over with him.

"Tired. But Carlito said you guys would be able to answer all of my questions."

Isa nodded, pulling up a seat next to his bed as Harrison grabbed one for Emerson. As she expected, Harrison stood, ever the intimidating warrior.

Arms crossed over his chest, he gave Graysen's lower calf a surprisingly gentle squeeze. "I'm glad to see you looking so good. And I'm sorry about—"

Graysen gave a sharp shake of his head. "No apologies. Carlito already told me what happened. I'm glad Grant and Belle's baby is healthy."

Harrison nodded, but that guilt still flickered across his expression. Not exactly surprising, since Isa knew he considered the people who worked under him more like his family. He took his job and his responsibility to his employees very seriously—as he should. It was why people rarely left Red Stone Security. Once you got a job with them, you didn't want to leave.

"What do you know so far?" Harrison asked.

Graysen lifted his good shoulder. "Carlito mainly asked questions about how everything went down. Wanted to get a timeline of when I took out each threat and on what floor. Sounds like it's a bit of a clusterfuck at Raptor."

Harrison snorted. "They're having a hell of a time with the crime scene."

"I bet. Listen, just tell me everything. Like how the hell Yuri Mikhailov was in the country, much less the building."

Isa hadn't known who he was, but now she knew that Yuri was a hacker/terrorist who was wanted by Interpol and a whole mess of agencies.

"The Feds are going crazy over the fact that he was in the country." Her boss shook his head, his expression grim. "He approached Persky with a deal—to input code into the computer programming for multiple drones under contract by the US government. The drones would operate like normal until they crossed into specific territories. Yuri, or someone working with him, had them configured it so that once they crossed certain physical coordinates, he would be able to commandeer the drones into his command. He could have started a war—or multiple wars—with them. And it would appear that they were under US control."

Graysen frowned. "How did Persky get involved with them though? He wasn't even on our radar. Or the government's radar. Was he?"

Harrison shook his head. "He wasn't on anyone's radar. The Russians approached him and offered him a lot of money. He has—had—an ex-wife, alimony, and debt. It appears as if he wanted to leave his life behind, and start over somewhere new. Not only that...he had a new girlfriend. A young one, who was pushing him to give her the kind of lifestyle she was accustomed to and to run away with him."

Graysen's frown deepened. "She with the Russians?"

Isa nodded. "Yes. And he was an idiot for thinking a woman like her would ever fall for him." Isa had seen the pictures from the file the police had, and the woman who'd targeted Persky had been beyond stunning. As in 'Angelina Jolie and Megan Fox combined' level of hotness. Whereas Persky was not unattractive, but he was middle-aged and out of shape.

Harrison grunted in agreement.

"Why'd they lock down the building like that?" Graysen asked.

"He overheard my conversation with Emerson. Had the line tapped." Isa gritted her teeth at her own stupidity. She'd been vague in what she'd told Emerson, but clearly not enough so.

"He jumped the gun and called Yuri, from the looks of it," Harrison continued. "Yuri already had men in place on site while they wrapped up their operation. They only had one more bit of code to input and it had to be on site, since the programs weren't linked to any outside sources. Yuri simply shut down the building, blocked the exits and killed anyone who got in their way. The place was supposed to be empty that late, but there were a few stragglers. Not to mention Hamilton's actual security team."

Guilt bubbled up inside Isa at the mention of the innocent people who'd been killed. If she'd never called Emerson, maybe they'd all still be alive. Their families wouldn't be mourning right now.

Harrison's mouth curved up into a hard smile. "What they didn't count on was a highly trained former CIA operative taking them out one by one."

"Hell," Graysen murmured, shaking his head.

"From what the couple remaining men who lived through everything had to tell the police, they planned to kill Persky anyway. *He* obviously didn't know that."

"What was their original plan, before things went sideways?"

"Persky planned to continue working for Raptor for a few weeks before putting in his notice of retirement. After searching his place, the cops found multiple fake identities. Looks as if he planned to leave the country, start over as someone else. No one would have ever known about the embedded code. Later they might have figured it out, but it would have been too late to do anything about it. If not for you guys," Harrison said, looking between the three of them, "they'd have gotten away with it."

Isa was still trying to wrap her mind around everything. After the way her father had betrayed their country, betrayed her, she knew what people were capable of. But it was still hard to swallow what Persky had planned to do. "Oh, and Shawn Grady was working on Persky's authority to add that tracking software to my computer."

The police and Feds were still trying to figure out if Grady was complicit in Persky's whole scheme or just following orders of his VP. So far he was just in custody but hadn't been charged with anything yet.

When she noticed how pale Graysen was, she squeezed his hand once, then stood. "All right guys, it's time for Graysen to get some rest." He didn't protest so she knew she was right.

After the others were gone, she resumed her place next to his bed, still holding his hand.

"What do you need? Are you hungry? I can probably sneak in some food so you don't have to eat what comes out of the hospital kitchen."

He shifted slightly, tried to hide a wince.

"Graysen, don't move. I'll get whatever—"

"I want an answer to my question."

She raised her eyebrows. "What question?"

"Did you mean it when you said you loved me?" The desperation in his gaze took her off guard.

Her heart turned over. "Yes. I truly get why you did what you did. Before everything went crazy on Thursday, Mara gave me a file on my father. One you've apparently been sitting on for a very long time. Why didn't you tell me he got Colby killed?" Tears burned her eyes at the reminder that her father had been behind the execution of one of Graysen's best friends. Graysen had never told her, not even when he'd been trying to get her to forgive him.

He cupped her cheek with his good hand, his grip gentle as he stroked his thumb over her cheek. "I didn't want you to know that. He'd already hurt you so much, but he was still your father. I didn't want to destroy whatever love you still had for him."

She swallowed hard, not bothering to blink back the tears now. "I wasn't ready to listen to you a year ago, wasn't ready to face the truth that my father was a monster. But I love you. I've never stopped loving you, even if I wanted to deny it. And I've missed you so damn much." Her voice cracked on the last word. She could have easily lost him.

His grip tightened slightly and she leaned down, erasing the distance between them. The instant her lips brushed against his, the spark of awareness flared out to all her nerve endings. A simple kiss shouldn't have this much effect on her, but Graysen West was alive and relatively well.

She couldn't let Graysen go. Simply couldn't do it. He'd risked his life to save hers and he was one of the best men she'd ever known. She was going to hold on to him tight and never let go.

CHAPTER TWENTY

Saturday night

"I feel almost guilty having a good time while Graysen is in the hospital." Emerson tightened her fingers around Carlito's.

He hadn't been sure if she'd want to even come out tonight but was glad she had. They'd been in and out of the hospital all day Friday and most of today just waiting for Graysen to be able to take visitors. "Visiting hours were over and Isa was staying with him. There's nothing we could have done but sit in the waiting room overnight." And that wasn't his idea of a good time with Emerson. Not when he was dying to get her back to his place, strip her naked and get inside her. He'd been thinking of doing that since they'd been freed Thursday—okay, for the past six months.

"I know. Still..." She trailed off, smiled as he opened the door to his truck for her.

He planned to put an even bigger smile on her face tonight. As he strapped her in, he brushed his lips over hers, deepened the kiss for just a second before pulling back. Her lips were glossy as she looked up at him. Growling, he shut the door and rounded to the driver's side. They'd be home soon.

"So what did you think of the parade?" The annual Christmas boat parade was something he'd only gone to a couple times and that had been years ago, and never with a date. He hadn't even wanted to go tonight, but after what Emerson had been through, he'd wanted to give her a sense of normalcy in her life again.

"I loved it." She reached over, linked her fingers with his as he steered his way through the packed parking lot.

He loved that she didn't hold back with her affection. Now that they were officially together, she made it clear to everyone that she was his and vice versa. It eased an ache inside him he hadn't realized had been so deep. Still, he was counting down until he had a ring on her finger. Then the whole damn world would know she was his.

"You know, I have a friend who got, uh, intimate with her now-husband at that parade."

He glanced over to see her cheeks flushing that sexy shade of pink he adored. "*At* the parade?"

"Oh yeah. She's actually married to one of the guys at Red Stone. I couldn't believe it when she told me."

"Hmm."

"What?"

"Just thinking about the logistics of that—and wondering if you'd be quiet enough for me to stroke you to climax."

Just as he'd hoped, her cheeks flushed even darker. She cleared her throat. "Hopefully you'll find out if I'm quiet or loud soon enough."

He just grinned as he pulled out onto the main street, leaving the crowded parking lot of the park behind.

Green and red lights were strung up around trees and light poles all along this strip. "I plan to tonight."

Her breathing increased ever so slightly and just like that, his cock turned rock hard. Tonight was the first night of many with Emerson. The anticipation of stretching her out naked on his bed, of finally claiming her, of seeing every inch of her curves... He shifted uncomfortably.

When his work phone buzzed in his pocket, he bit back a curse. It might be nothing, but it was late enough that if he was getting a call, he was going to have to go in. With this huge case right now, he had no choice. Hell, he was lucky he'd been able to take a few hours off with her.

"It's work, isn't it?" she asked as he pulled his phone out.

Sighing, he nodded as he glanced at the screen. "Yeah."

He answered the call from his boss. Ten minutes later he ended it, more than frustrated.

"Don't worry about it," Emerson said as he set the phone on the center console. She'd heard enough of his half of the conversation to know he'd been called in. "Why don't you just drop me off at my place—"

"What did I say about that?"

She laughed lightly, the sound pure music. "Okay, okay. I was just giving you the option if you wanted it. I feel a little weird being at your place without you there."

He frowned, not liking that at all. His place was hers, as far as he was concerned. But he knew when to keep his mouth shut. Especially since he'd already pushed her into staying with him. Not that she'd pushed back but... He didn't want to give her a reason to leave.

After getting her settled into his place and double-checking that she would set the alarm, he headed to the station. Apparently the Feds were there and wanted to talk to him. Again. Something told him it was going to be a long night.

* * *

Carlito stared at Emerson sleeping on his couch. He'd been gone almost six hours so he hadn't expected her to still be awake. A blanket was tucked around her, but one foot was sticking out, showing her painted red toenails with little white snowmen on her big toes. Everything about her was adorable. *Yep, never letting her go.* It might have only been six months since he first met her, but he felt as if he'd been waiting for this woman for a lifetime. As if she'd been made just for him.

She must have been exhausted since she didn't even hear him come in and disarm the security system. Moving slowly, he lifted the blanket off her—froze when he realized she was just wearing one of his T-shirts, then scooped her up. She was lean and leggy, and he loved the feel of her up against him. Knew he'd never tire of it, of her. Protectiveness like he'd never known surged through him as he held her close. He had the insane urge to keep her close to him all the time after what had happened Thursday. Yeah, he knew it would pass, but right now he was in overprotective mode.

She made a soft moaning sound and shifted against him. Her blue eyes opened, her expression softening. "Hey," she murmured, laying her head on his shoulder as she curled into him. "What time is it?"

"A little after three." He'd done everything in his power to get back to her as soon as he could.

"I tried to wait up."

He nudged his bedroom door open with his foot, his cock hard at just the feel of her in his arms. He'd been restraining himself for six damn months, pretending he just wanted friendship. That was all over now. Now she was going to have no doubt how much he wanted her. He felt almost possessed with the need to have her, claim her. After everything that had happened Thursday, he guessed part of his blinding need was because he kept reminding himself she was safe with him.

The wood slat blinds over the windows let in enough light for him to see, even though he had the layout of his room memorized.

He stretched her out on the middle of his bed before switching on the bathroom light. He'd waited a long time for this and he wasn't going to be cheated out of seeing all of her completely bared to him. Every. Single. Inch.

She made a cute little sound as she arched her back, stretching her hands over her head. "You, naked, now." Her voice was as sleepy as her expression.

He grinned at her words, loving this side of her. It didn't take him long to strip off his service weapon and clothes. The only thing he left on was his boxers. Because once those were off, he'd have no control left.

Crawling onto the bed, he spread her thighs as he moved in between them, gliding his hands over her smooth legs.

She shivered, moaned softly as he reached under her T-shirt and tugged at her panties. He liked not being able to see what she had on under, to just feel. When he pulled away a skimpy black scrap of material that was mostly lace, he knew for certain that very soon he was going to ask her to model for him in various stages of undress.

Now the only thing that mattered was tasting her.

"Been thinking about doing this for so long," he murmured, moving until he had her completely caged in beneath him.

"What kinds of things did you imagine doing?" Her grin was wicked as she smoothed her hands up his chest and over his shoulders.

He shuddered at the feel of her touching him. She hadn't even gotten close to his cock and he was ready to come. Yeah, he needed to slow things down. This woman got him more turned on than he'd ever been, just by existing.

"Burying my face between your legs while you were sitting at your desk at work...when anyone could walk in." The truth was he'd never risk anyone seeing her in that state, but it was something he'd fantasized about more than once.

He crushed his mouth over hers before she could respond, savored the way she arched up against him. He could have lost her this week, less than thirty-six hours ago. If she'd gone without him, hadn't thought to call him... He broke out in a sweat just thinking about that. They both needed this.

She wrapped her legs around his waist as he teased his tongue past her lips. When she dug her fingers into his back and started grinding against him, he pulled back, breathing hard. At this rate, he'd be inside her in seconds.

They'd already had "the talk" and were both clean, so he wasn't using a condom. Something he was eternally grateful for. Getting to be inside Emerson without any barriers was his idea of heaven.

She watched him with heavy-lidded eyes as she trailed her fingers down his chest, over his abdomen—he sucked in a sharp breath, rolled his hips back. *Nope.*

"Not yet, darlin'." He simply didn't trust himself, and she deserved a hell of a lot of foreplay.

She pouted a little until he stripped her T-shirt off— and he sucked in another breath.

Fantasizing about her and seeing her bared to him were two very different things. As if drawn by a magnet, he reached out, cupped one full breast. Shuddering hunger sparked in her gaze.

He wanted more of that from her. Wanted everything from her.

Slowly, he teased a thumb over her nipple, watching the pink bud harden even more.

She squirmed against the bed, tightened her legs around him as he began teasing her other nipple. Her breathing grew even more erratic, her face flushed as he oh so slowly ran his thumbs around her nipples, making her hitch in a breath. He could watch her forever.

"You are perfect," he murmured. His cock was heavy between his legs, but he ignored it.

"And you are a giant tease." Her voice was raspy and uneven.

He could tease her even longer, but that would mean depriving both of them. *Not happening.* Leaning down, he took one of her nipples in his mouth, sucked.

The action seemed to set her off. Groaning, she arched her back, trying to push herself deeper into his mouth as he gently pressed his teeth down.

She slid her fingers through his hair, cupped his head tight. "Touch me between my legs." The words were part demand, part plea.

He slid his hand down her stomach, moving slowly until he cupped her mound. She had the barest amount of fine, blonde hair there. She rolled her hips against his hand, the action sensual.

All the muscles in his body were pulled taut as he traced a finger down her slick folds. She was so wet. For him. *Hell, yeah.*

Feeling how turned on she was made it hard to think straight. "I'm not letting you go, Emerson." The words ripped from him as he slipped a finger inside her. Christ, she was tight. *So damn tight.*

He knew it had been a while for her—as it had been for him. Even before he'd met her. He'd seen what his best friend had with his wife, saw what his sisters had, and he wanted it too. He'd just never thought he'd actually meet someone he wanted forever with until Emerson.

"Good. Not letting you go either." She moaned, rolled her hips as he slid another finger inside her.

Desperate to taste her, to bring her to climax, he leaned down, began feathering kisses along her abdomen. Her inner walls tightened around his fingers the farther down he moved.

His cock jerked once as he thought about what she'd feel like once he slid inside her.

Her clit was swollen, peeking out from her folds. He closed his eyes for a long moment, inhaled her sweet scent. He wanted to remember everything about this moment. The day he made Emerson his forever.

When he flicked his tongue over her sensitive bundle of nerves, she jerked against his face, an excited moan tearing from her.

"Carlito." The sound of her saying his name, all breathy and needy, made him crazy. And determined to have her shout it as she came against his face.

He increased the pressure against her clit, stroking her over and over as she writhed against his face.

"Yes, yes…" She dug her fingers into his scalp as she moved closer to the edge.

He had no doubt she was close, could feel the way her inner walls tightened around his fingers faster and faster. Her hips rolled against his face, wild and erratic.

"About to come," she rasped out.

He laved his tongue against her, harder and harder until her back arched and her inner walls clenched convulsively around his fingers. Her climax seemed to slam through her. He didn't stop until he'd wrenched every bit of pleasure from her, until she was lying boneless against his sheets.

On his bed. Right where she belonged.

He lifted his head, felt pure male satisfaction at her sated expression. She looked down the length of her body at him, her face flushed and her eyes a little dazed.

"I'm going to have a ring on your finger by New Year's." He figured he probably should have kept that to himself a *little* longer, but he'd almost lost her. Could easily lose her at any moment, and he wasn't going to waste a second of the time they had together.

More than most he knew how fragile life was. He saw death and what humans did to other humans every day. And he was locking her down, claiming her as soon as possible. A couple weeks seemed like long enough for her to get used to the idea.

She blinked once, quickly coming out of her daze, and pushed up so that she was sitting. "That better not be your idea of a proposal," she whispered. "Because it sucks." With a grin, she reached for his boxers, shoved them down his hips. By the time he'd gotten them fully off, she had her long fingers wrapped around his hard length.

"Not…a proposal," he managed to get out as she stroked him once, twice. Because he was going to do things right. It was old-fashioned and probably what she'd consider archaic, but he was still going to talk to her father first. But no matter what, his ring was going on her finger. If she'd have him.

"Good." She stared down at his erection as she continued stroking him, seemed pleased by what she saw.

And hell if that didn't make him feel a hundred feet tall. But he needed inside her now. Though he hated to stop her from touching him, even for a second, he lightly grasped her wrist, moved it away.

But he didn't let go. He guided her arm above her head, then the other one, and clasped her wrists together as he covered her body with his.

He could feel every inch of her nakedness underneath his. Her nipples beaded tightly against his chest and though he wanted to capture one in his mouth, he stayed where he was, kept his focus on her face. "I love you, Emerson." After what he'd just admitted he needed to say the damn words that he'd never said to any woman. He wasn't going to hide how he felt, deny what she was to him.

"I love you too." Even with the muted light streaming in, he could see her face clearly, could see she meant every word.

Her words wrapped around him, soothed the darkest edge of him. *She loves me back.* He crushed his mouth to hers as he repositioned himself at her entrance. He'd felt how slick she was, knew she was ready, but he still thrust inside her slowly. Savoring every second.

She gasped into his mouth, jerking her wrists against his hold. He decided to let go because he wanted to feel her fingers stroking over him.

As soon as he loosened his grip she wrapped her arms around him, dug her fingers into his back. She arched, tightening her grip on him as he began thrusting inside her.

This was what heaven was. Pure heaven. His balls pulled up tight as he drove into her, over and over.

He forced himself not to come yet, to hold off as he savored the feel of her tight walls wrapped around him, the way her pliant body felt beneath him.

When she nipped at his bottom lip and slid her hands down until she was gripping his ass, he let go. A man only had so much control.

And Emerson had shredded the last of his.

Groaning, he tore his mouth from hers as he came. He slid his hand through her hair, cupped her head. He wanted to watch her, for her to see exactly how much she owned him.

Then he reached between their bodies and teased her already sensitive clit. A few gentle strokes, and it pushed her into another orgasm. Her inner walls clenched around his cock just as they'd done around his fingers.

But this was more intense. His own climax still punched through him, slamming against all his nerve endings as she found another release.

Though he wanted to watch her as she came, he buried his face against her neck, breathed in her scent as he emptied himself inside her. Eventually he stopped thrusting, lifted his head to look at her.

She had that sated look again as she cupped his face between her hands. "That was perfect." She brushed her lips against his and sighed in satisfaction as her head fell back against the pillow.

Slowly he pulled out of her, even as his cock protested. She was exactly where he wanted to be. Always. But he wanted to clean her up. First, however, he rolled onto his side and pulled her close.

She immediately curled into him, laying her head against his chest. "I'm pretty sure I could stay like this all night. Or all morning now, I suppose." She let out a little laugh at the last word.

"There's no reason we can't do that. I'm not going in later today." He'd already gotten approval from his boss. The Feds and the lead detective on the case were wrapping things up and they didn't need him. And if they did, his phone would be off. He had priorities.

"You sure you don't need to?"

"I'm sure. We're going to be naked the majority of the day. Just FYI."

She laughed against his chest. "Your bossiness really is going to take some getting used to."

He slid his hand down her spine and kept going until he reached her ass, squeezed once. "I think you like it."

"I definitely do." She nipped lightly at his chest and just like that, his cock started to lengthen again.

Oh yeah, they were in for a lot more naked time before they left this bed.

* * *

Emerson pressed mute on the television at the sound of Carlito's front door opening. He'd just left ten minutes ago and said he would be back in about thirty. He was getting them breakfast—well, technically a late lunch by this hour—since he had pretty much no food here. His refrigerator was just as bad as hers.

"You're back early," she called out from the living room. Stretched out on his couch, she hadn't moved since he'd left. The last few hours they'd made love multiple times and she was exhausted.

Happy, but exhausted.

"Emerson?"

She jerked up at the sound of a familiar voice. Two seconds later three very familiar faces came into view as Carlito's mom and two sisters stepped into the living room. Since she was just wearing a T-shirt and panties, and was in his house in the middle of the day on a Sunday, it was pretty clear they were more than just friends.

Camilla, who was thirty-seven years old, beamed then turned to her sister Gabriela and actually high-fived her. "I told you telling her that he was seeing someone would work."

Even though the T-shirt came to mid-thigh, Emerson still pulled the blanket tightly around her and stood. She felt really awkward being half dressed in his living room facing his family, but smiled at them. "Hey, guys. Carlito just went out for food. He didn't say you were stopping by."

His mom hurried over to her and pulled her into a tight hug. "He doesn't know we planned to stop by. But after seeing the news we wanted to come and check on him and he wasn't answering his phone."

Carlito had told her how his family sometimes stopped by unannounced, but he'd left out that they must have keys. "He's doing good. We both are." She narrowed her gaze on Camilla. "You lied to me about Carlito seeing someone?"

Camilla's face flushed a light shade of pink. "It was the only thing I could think of to get you to see him as more than a friend. It was…"

"Totally wrong?"

Her cheeks turned darker as her sister nudged her. "It worked, right?"

Emerson just shook her head. What had worked was Carlito finally just asking her out. But she didn't say that. "So…do you all want coffee or anything?" She was pretty sure that was all Carlito had anyway.

His mother, Ariana, shook her head and sat on the couch Emerson had just been on. She patted it and motioned for Emerson to sit as Carlito's sisters both sat on a loveseat.

Feeling a little like she was under a microscope as the women all watched her almost expectantly, Emerson sat—even if she really wanted to go put on pants. Or real clothes that weren't rumpled and didn't smell like sex.

"So when did this happen?" Gabriela finally spoke. Of the two sisters, she was always the quietest. And that was a relative term. Because his family was pretty loud.

"Ah, well, Thursday night." She wasn't going to go into details about everything that had happened. The news had gotten some of it right, but they had no idea how bad everything had been, what could have happened with those drones. Unfortunately her name had been released to the media today as one of the survivors of the terrorist attack.

"And?" His mother's eyebrows rose.

"And what?" She wasn't sure what they wanted to know. Surely they couldn't want details about their relationship. Emerson had grown up with a father who'd treated her more like a son than a daughter. She'd constantly been surrounded by her father's friends. Which was more than fine with her—she loved the way she'd been raised. But she didn't have many girlfriends, and the ones she did have, well, they didn't really talk about sex and relationships. Most of her friends she talked computers and gaming with.

"When are you two tying the knot?"

Emerson choked on air at his mother's blunt question. "I, ah… I need clothes." She jumped up and hurried from the room, the laughter of the three women trailing after her.

She took her time in Carlito's room, washing her face, brushing her teeth and changing into the clothes she'd worn over here last night. Jeans and a sweater. Better than being half naked. Feeling more prepared to deal with his family, she headed back out there to find the three of them all had mugs of coffee and were sitting in roughly the same place she'd left them.

"We decided to make coffee," Ariana said. "Grab a cup and join us."

Nodding, she did just that and once again found herself under the microscope of three nosy, beautiful women. They might be intimidating but she loved the idea that soon she'd be part of this wonderful family.

"We need babies in our life again," Camilla said abruptly.

Emerson just nodded, hoping the woman wasn't talking about her and Carlito. Thankfully, she heard the front door open and internally sighed. Carlito was back to save her!

Her sister nodded, as if what Camilla had said was normal. "All our kids are pre-teens or teens. So it's up to you and Carlito to give us all babies."

She stared at the three of them in slight horror as Carlito stepped into the room. He gave his mom and sisters each a quick kiss before sliding onto the couch next to her. To her surprise, he pulled her into his lap, wrapped his arm securely around her waist.

"You're ambushing my Emerson about babies already?"

Camilla nodded. "You better believe it. We need cuteness and kids who don't talk back or think they know more than us. Or roll their eyes at us every time they look at us."

"As soon as she lets me, I'll be putting babies in her," Carlito murmured.

Emerson jerked in his hold, turned to stare at his wicked, wicked expression. The man was loving this. And she was going to kill him later.

The three women dissolved into laughter, either from his words or her horrified expression, and started talking amongst themselves about some Christmas party.

"You're insane," she whispered.

"True. But so's my family. Now you see what you're getting into. And it's too late to run now," he murmured, his grip tightening. "I told you. By New Year's."

He'd surprised her last night with that. Sort of. She'd known he was serious, but all the talk of putting a ring on her finger had definitely surprised her—and pleased her. After what they'd survived, she wasn't wasting a second of her life. And the thought of being engaged and eventually married to the sexiest, sweetest man she knew? Why would she run from that? She wanted the world to know he was hers too.

They'd talk about the whole baby thing later when they didn't have an audience. She wanted a few years of just them first, but then... Yeah, the idea of having a mini Carlito made her heart melt.

"I expect a real proposal." Her words were just for his ears.

The heated look he gave her told her he'd do it right. She couldn't wait to see what he came up with. Because she didn't care about the ring or having a flashy proposal. She just wanted something real, that came from the heart. And she knew without a doubt Carlito would do that.

CHAPTER TWENTY-ONE

Three weeks later

Graysen was about to lose his mind. Isa had been taking care of him for the last few weeks and he hated that she seemed to see him as some sort of invalid. He was just fine now. Okay, his ribs ached, but who gave a crap about that? All the important parts were working, especially his cock.

It had been over a year since he'd been inside her. He was done waiting.

Stretched out on her bed, he called her cell phone, knowing he was probably driving her a little crazy by this point. He knew where she was, but was anxious for her to get back home. She'd refused to let him go with her, insisting that he needed rest. Screw rest. He needed to be buried inside her as deep as he could get. Mark her. Brand her as his, forever.

"Hey, babe," she answered on the third ring, breathless.

"Where are you?"

"I…don't want to tell you."

Shoving straight up in bed, he frowned. "What's wrong?"

She sighed. "Nothing. I'm just in the driveway unloading all the groceries. I knew if I told you, you'd want to come help. And I think you need to take it easy."

He gritted his teeth. *Take it easy, my ass.*

He took a deep breath and ordered himself not to get out there and help her bring everything inside. It would just drive her even crazier and put her on edge. And right now, he wanted her in a good mood. Because he had a plan. "I'm actually feeling a little winded." He didn't even feel bad for lying.

"Were you doing something while I was gone?" Her voice was slightly admonishing. He'd never realized how much she could worry.

He liked how much she cared about him, that he finally had her back in his life. But he wasn't a child or an invalid. Very soon he planned to remind her that he was a man. *Her* man.

The last three weeks he'd been mostly laid up at her place. They'd both been forced to take paid vacation from Red Stone—courtesy of Harrison, who'd been insistent that as long as Graysen was home, then Isa was too. *God bless that man.* Graysen might be going crazy on virtual bed rest but at least he got to spend time with the woman he loved.

Now he was past ready for sex. He was dying for it.

Dying to taste her again. They'd made out a lot, but she always put on the brakes, worried she'd hurt him. She was so damn worried about his ribs that neither of them had had an orgasm in the past few weeks. He was frustrated, and even though she wasn't acting like it, he imagined she was sexually frustrated too.

"I took Peaches for a walk and lifted weights," he lied. He'd walked the dog but there had been no weight lifting. He was saving all his energy for Isa.

There was a tense silence and he guessed she was tempering her response. She cleared her throat. "Where is Peaches, anyway?"

He could hear her moving around the kitchen now, had to resist going in to help her. "I dropped her off for a doggy play date next door after her walk." Because he wanted alone time with Isa with absolutely no interruptions. That included their dog, who didn't understand they needed personal time that didn't include her. And he didn't want Peaches staring at them or clawing at the door trying to get to them.

"Okay. I've got a few more bags to bring in. I'll come see you when I've got everything put up."

"Okay." When she walked in, she'd find him completely naked. He'd planned for her to find him in bed. Now, however... He swung his legs off the bed, twisted back and forth, stretching out. His ribs twinged, but man, he'd definitely been hurt worse. He'd had his femur snapped during a mission that involved jumping out of a plane. This was nothing compared to that.

And nothing was stopping him from being inside Isa in the next half hour. Maybe sooner than that. They didn't have to do acrobatics or anything, but they were both getting off.

At this point he'd settle for just her getting off. Yeah, he wanted to so bad he could taste it. He needed to bring her to climax, to see that sated expression on her face and know he'd put it there. She'd done so much for him, had let him back into her life.

The need was making him too damn edgy.

He made his way to the shower, turned it on and waited until steam billowed out before entering the stone and glass enclosure. Stepping under the hot jets, he savored the way they felt hitting his back. He was getting too damn stiff staying in that bed—and Isa was worse than any drill sergeant he'd ever had. She was so sweet and caring about her desire to make sure he stayed in bed—but there was absolutely no arguing with her. The woman was tough.

"Graysen?" Her sweet voice filled the room as he finished washing his hair.

"In here." He was already hard and aching for her.

"Why didn't you wait for me? I would have helped you." She stepped up to the enclosure, hands on hips.

He drank in the sight of her—wearing far too many clothes. "You got your cell phone on you?"

She blinked. "No."

Moving lightning fast, he opened the door and reached for her, dragged her into the shower with him.

She let out a yelp of protest right before he crushed his mouth over hers. He pushed her back against the slick wall, grinding up against her.

Moaning, she wrapped her arms around his neck, meeting his tongue stroke for stroke. He noticed she was careful to avoid touching the scarred, tender area on his shoulder. The hunger and need from her was palpable, letting him know she wanted him as badly as he wanted her.

Thank fuck.

"Clothes, off," he growled against her mouth, only pulling back long enough to start stripping her.

"Graysen, are you sure—"

He tugged her soaked sweater over her head, then started on her jeans. Soon she was completely naked, her wet clothes tossed out of the shower. Staring at her, he slid his hands down over her waist, then hips, and back up again. Her light brown nipples were rock hard, her chest falling and rising erratically as she drank in the sight of him.

Even when they'd slept together she'd stayed fully clothed. It was like she was trying to spare him the torture of seeing her but not being able to have her.

No more.

"If you start to feel—"

"I'll let you know." He cupped her cheek with one hand. "My stitches are out and I'm good. I need you, Isa."

Whatever she saw in his eyes must have convinced her because she nodded and for the first time in weeks he saw true, raw hunger. Maybe she'd been keeping it locked down for his sake, but it was all out in the open now. Just like when they'd been together before. She'd always been so sensual with him, so open and free.

"I need you too."

"I haven't been with anyone since you. For the record. And I don't want to know if you have or haven't. I just needed you to know—"

"I haven't either. Couldn't stand the thought of anyone else touching me." She grasped his cock, stroked once, twice before dropping to her knees in a fluid movement.

Elation pumped through him.

Hell, yeah. He hadn't been lying—he hadn't wanted to know either way. But to know she hadn't been with anyone either... Okay, who was he kidding? He was ecstatic.

This was supposed to be about her, but— He groaned as her lips wrapped around his hard length. He shuddered, buried a hand in her wet hair and held on.

Water cascaded down around them, her dark hair slick against her head as she took him fully in her mouth. She gripped the base of his cock hard, held firm as she teased the ultra-sensitive crown.

She knew exactly how to work him, exactly how to tease him until he was begging for more.

Leaning back against the wall he closed his eyes, lost himself in the sensation of her mouth. Deep down in a place he didn't want to acknowledge existed he'd been terrified that they'd never work things out, that he'd never get to experience the sweetness of Isa again.

To be here, at her mercy, with her perfect mouth on him—this was heaven and even better than he remembered. More intense. He rolled his hips as she went deeper. And when she sucked hard again, he knew he was close.

He tangled his hand in her hair, squeezed once before he could get any words out. "Isa, hold off."

She paused, gazed up at him, looking every inch the goddess she was. Her grin was wickedly sensual as she ignored his demand and started to lean back down.

But he tightened his grip. His ribs twinged as his breathing increased, but he didn't care about the discomfort. He was hanging on by a thread, and considering how long it had been since he'd been with anyone—since Isa, over a year ago—he wasn't coming in her mouth. Not this first time.

With a mock pout, she rose to her feet. "I've missed doing that," she murmured, going up on tiptoe and brushing her lips over his. "And I want to finish." Her voice was sexy, sultry.

He had her back against the wall in seconds. Chest to chest, hip to hip—he'd needed this on every level.

Her full, bare breasts pressed against him. The feel of her nipples gliding against him made his brain short-circuit. He cupped one soft mound, shuddered even as she did the same under his touch. He hadn't forgotten how sensitive she was. Had been fantasizing about this for so damn long.

She hitched a leg around his waist, rolling her hips against him. His cock throbbed, the ache flowing through him intense.

His chest was tight, and yeah, he was already feeling a little exhausted, but the adrenaline pumping through him kept him going. Hell, *Isa* kept him going.

Somehow he tore his mouth from hers. "Gotta taste you once." She was his addiction and he'd be damned if he didn't get at least one taste of her before he buried himself inside her.

"Graysen…" She sucked in a breath as he cupped her between her legs, slid a finger against her slick folds.

"Missed your pussy," he murmured, loving the way she blushed crimson. She'd never been a dirty talker and he loved working her up with words.

She dug her fingers into his waist, rolled her hips again, the action jerky. "What else did you miss?" she rasped out.

"Bringing you to climax with my mouth. Bending you over the edge of any surface we could find and fucking you until we were both boneless."

Her eyes closed as she let out a long, breathy moan. "I've missed that dirty mouth."

Smiling, he dipped his head to her throat and feathered kisses along the column of her neck. Her body was slick from the water rushing over them. She slid her hands up his chest and over his shoulders. When she dug her fingers into him, he began a slow path of kisses down her body, stopping at each breast to lavish them with attention.

As he flicked his tongue around her nipple, he continued stroking between her legs. But not enough that she'd climax. Not yet.

Still, he wanted her worked up and ready to combust by the time he got inside her. As he began to kneel down, she started to protest.

He ignored her. He knew his body's limits and nothing was stopping him from putting his mouth on her.

She didn't protest too hard. Once he was kneeling directly in front of her, she lifted a leg, propped her foot on the built-in tile bench—spreading herself wide for him.

When he met her gaze up the length of her body, all he saw was heat and hunger. His cock throbbed, aching to be inside her. But not until she was ready for him.

She slid her fingers through his hair the second before he buried his face between her legs. He'd already felt how slick she was and he wanted her on edge just like he was. So close she could barely take it.

As he teased his tongue along her slick folds, her fingers tightened ever so slightly. She was sweet, just like he remembered. Everything about her was seared into his memory. Including the sounds she made when they were naked and he was anywhere near her pussy.

The memories had haunted him pretty much every night over the last year.

He felt almost drunk on her taste. Focusing on her clit, he applied enough pressure to bring her right to the cusp of climax, but not reach it.

"You're such a tease." Her words were unsteady as she rolled her hips against his face. When she lowered her leg from the bench and tried to squeeze her thighs together he grasped one, held her legs open and continued teasing her. He loved her this way. Desperate. Needy.

She struggled against his hold, trying to find relief, but he kept going, on and on until he knew she was close. And he was going to feel her climax around his cock.

She was his prize for not dying weeks ago.

Eyes slightly dazed, she stared down at him. "You're stopping?"

"We're coming together." His words were a growled promise.

He pushed to his feet and for a second, swayed. *No.* He wasn't going to fail at this. He couldn't. Before he could move, she took over, pushing him onto the bench. Because he needed to sit, he let her move him.

Crawling on top of him, she grasped his cock and pushed up on her knees. He held her hips tight, steadying her as she positioned herself over his hard length. Closing his eyes, he rubbed his cheek between her breasts as she simply hovered over him—teasing him as he'd teased her. It wouldn't take much effort to thrust upward, to completely fill her. But he liked the anticipation. He could spend all damn night touching her everywhere, relearning every inch of her body.

"I'm so close, baby," she murmured. "Not gonna last once you're in me." She eased down on him. Slowly.

He sucked in a breath. Damn, she was as tight as he remembered. His balls pulled up hard and his brain short-circuited with every inch she moved lower until he filled her completely.

"I can't live without you, Isa," he whispered, looking into her eyes, his entire body on fire. Water pounded down around them and for this moment it felt like they were the only two people in the world.

"Good thing you won't have to. I'm not going anywhere."

"Marry me." All his muscles tightened as he held back from coming.

She blinked and he rolled his hips, thrusting upward. She jolted at the sensation, gripped his shoulders tight. "You can't...propose while you're inside me."

"I just did. Marry me next week. I don't want to spend another day without you as my wife." His voice was rough, every muscle tense with the need to drive into her until he came.

"Graysen." She moaned as he thrust again, her inner walls clenching tighter and tighter.

Oh yeah, she was close. And he was going to push her over the edge. But not yet. "I'll do this all night. Say yes and you can come."

Laughing lightly, she nipped at his bottom lip. Now he was the one moaning into her mouth.

"Say yes," he demanded, barely hanging on.

She gently traced the area around his mostly healed chest wound before whispering, "Yes."

He jolted at her simple response. When he looked in her eyes he saw the woman he loved more than anything, the woman he wanted to have kids with, to grow old with. The woman he was never letting go.

Reaching between their bodies, he massaged her clit, adding the right amount of pressure to push her over the edge.

As soon as he started rubbing her, she began riding him. And he was done for. Gritting his teeth, he held off coming until her inner walls started convulsing rapidly around him.

He sought out her mouth as she cried out his name, claiming her as she claimed him right back. She rode him fast and hard as they both found their release.

He had to tear his mouth from hers as his climax crested. Burying his face against her neck, he completely let go of his control.

She was the only woman he'd ever been able to let his walls down around. His sweet Isa, who was crying out his name as she continued riding him.

Eventually they both stilled, and though he was ready to collapse he held her tight to him, his face still buried against her neck. The steam billowed around them, the flowing water providing a soothing sound to the backdrop of their labored breaths. "I'm probably going to say this a lot the next few months, but I love you."

She smiled against his shoulder. "Pretty sure I can live with that. Because I love you too. And we've got a lot of time to make up for," she murmured. "A year's worth of sex, on top of all the regular sex we'll be having."

He laughed, his chest rumbling, and though the tightness and discomfort was there from his wound, it felt good to laugh. To have the woman he loved naked and in his arms.

Next week he was going to make her his wife. Best way he could think of to start the new year—and the rest of their lives together.

EPILOGUE

Valentine's Day

Lizzy Caldwell slid into her husband's lap, wrapped her arm around his broad shoulders as she looked out at the crowd of people in Belle and Grant's backyard. Grant and Belle had decided to throw a last-minute barbeque at their place for the Red Stone crew even though their baby was only two months old. Lizzy wouldn't have been so welcoming to people that early into motherhood, but Belle was taking this whole motherhood thing a heck of a lot better than Lizzy had at first.

The weather was chilly, sunny and perfect for outside relaxing. The grill had tons of food on it and the scent of barbeque filled the air. Someone had strung up red and pink paper hearts so they crisscrossed over the pool and the patio area.

She'd never imagined that when she started working for Red Stone Security, and eventually married one of the owners, her family would grow quite as much as it had.

Porter nuzzled her neck for a moment and she let out a sigh.

"Everyone's having a great time," she murmured. "Apparently we all needed this."

"No kidding." His gaze strayed to their son, Maddox, who was almost two and was toddling around everywhere.

Porter's brother Harrison stood near Maddox, acting like a mother bear whenever he got too close to the pool. Around Maddox or his own wife was the only time Harrison seemed to have a soft side, and it made Lizzy love her brother-in-law all the more for it. "You think Mara and Harrison will ever have kids?"

"Nah. I don't think they want them."

"I don't think so either." Mara was one of Lizzy's closest friends but she'd never talked about wanting kids. Her husband was the same. Lizzy snorted. "Do you remember how terrified she looked when we first handed her Maddox when he was a baby?"

Porter laughed, burying his face against her neck for a long moment that she cherished. His big body shook, the rumble of laughter coming from him music to her ears. "It was like we'd given her a bomb."

"They're good with Maddox though. And Athena." Belle and Grant's new baby. "Well...let's hope they're ready for a new niece or nephew to spoil," she whispered in his ear. Not that it mattered. There were about forty or fifty people milling around the backyard, all drinking, laughing and talking.

Porter stiffened slightly and pulled back to look at her. "Are you saying..."

Grinning, she brushed her lips over his. "Yeah. Got the official yes from the doctor this morning." She'd been feeling nauseous the past couple weeks and had missed her period so she'd gone to see her doctor—even though she'd been pretty certain she was pregnant. Once you'd gone through it, it wasn't a feeling you forgot.

He crushed his mouth to hers hard despite the crowd around them. Porter was the silent type, but he'd never shied away from affection. He looked like he'd just won the lottery when he pulled back from her. "How are you feeling?" Suddenly his face morphed into a mask of concern.

"Really good. No more nausea—for now, at least." Last time it had come and gone throughout her entire pregnancy. This time she hoped it stayed far away.

"How long until we tell everyone?"

"Maybe another four weeks. I want to get through the first trimester."

Still grinning, he simply nodded.

"Hey, you two," Belle said, coming to sit on the cushioned bench next to them, sleeping baby in her arms. "You look like you're up to something." Her gaze narrowed as she glanced between the two of them.

"Just enjoying ourselves," Porter said.

Belle gave him a look that said she wasn't sure she believed him, but continued. "I was worried Athena wouldn't be able to sleep with all these people around but she's been out for three hours."

Lizzy grinned. "I remember those days. Eat, sleep, poop. Repeat."

Laughing, Belle nodded. "Pretty much." When she looked at her little girl, her expression was filled with so much love.

Lizzy was overjoyed that Grant had found Belle. He'd been through so much, only to fall in love with one of the sweetest women ever. "How much does your cousin love that you named your baby after her?"

Now Belle rolled her eyes. "For the record, it wasn't after her. I just love the name, but that doesn't matter to her. She's rubbing it in to pretty much everyone in our family."

Lizzy's gaze strayed to where Athena and Quinn were talking with Travis and Noel—whose little guy was fifteen months old. It was hard to believe how many little ones were running around now. Just three years ago none of her friends had kids. Now it seemed over half of them did. And she loved it.

Loved every second of her crazy life. Going to work for Red Stone Security had changed her world in so many ways. Ways she'd forever be grateful for.

"So guess who I'm pretty sure is pregnant?" Belle whispered conspiratorially. Before either of them could ask who, she said, "Jordan and Vincent. I think, at least." Yawning, she looked across their big yard at said couple.

Vincent had Jordan sitting on his lap on a lounger near the pool, one of his big hands draped protectively over her slightly protruding stomach. The loose sweater she had on probably didn't hide her belly as much as she thought it did.

"Yeah, I kinda figured," Porter murmured. "He's been more growly than normal today to anyone who gets too close to her."

Lizzy just snorted. Vincent was ridiculous when it came to Jordan. Once upon a time Lizzy had thought he was a dog. The man had been such a player. Now that she knew the truth about what had happened between him and Jordan so many years ago—how she'd gone into WITSEC without telling him, breaking his heart—it was good to see him so settled. Even if he was insanely protective. "Sweet Lord, help Jordan if she has a baby girl."

Porter barked out a laugh at that, startling baby Athena, who gurgled and opened those gorgeous blue eyes.

Immediately she tucked her head into Belle's chest, opening her little mouth and making smacking sounds. Lizzy snickered. "Someone's hungry."

"This angel is always eating," Belle murmured, pulling her nursing cover over her chest and Athena's little body. "You guys mind?"

Lizzy shook her head. "Of course not... Did I hear through the grapevine that Carlito proposed to Emerson using the rookies at the PD?"

Laughing, Belle nodded. "Oh yeah. They all held up signs with one letter each and were waiting on the beach where he took her for the proposal. And it took him forever to pick out the ring. Guess who he wanted to drag around with him to stores for his mission—a month after I gave birth? I about killed him." She adjusted Athena slightly under the cover as the baby fed.

"I can't believe he didn't just ask one of his sisters."

"That's what I said. But apparently they've been making him crazy wanting babies. He begged me and I just couldn't say no."

"Sounds about right." Lizzy's gaze strayed for a second as she spotted Isa and Graysen arriving. They were late but it was good to see them. Lizzy loved seeing Isa so dang happy. "Graysen's doing good."

Porter snorted softly. "Yeah, and going crazy on desk duty. I think Harrison's about to send him back out into the field."

"With Isa?"

"Yeah. He thinks they'll make a good team, and after their last job, nothing can be as bad as that."

"I hope not. That was crazy," Belle murmured. As she lifted her nursing cover off, she set Athena on her shoulder and stood. "I need some food but I'll see you guys later."

Lizzy started to stand when Reece, her friend Charlotte's little boy, came racing out of a cluster of people, two cupcakes in his hands and a face covered in pink and red icing. Kell, his giant of a father, was five steps behind him. He scooped the little guy up—and got a face full of cupcake.

"It feels wrong to laugh," Lizzy said, pushing to her feet even as a chuckle burst out of her. "I'm going to grab something to drink. You want another beer?" she asked Porter.

He shook his head, standing. "Nah. Gotta pick my dad up from the airport in a couple hours. I'll stick to sweet tea for now."

She linked her fingers through Porter's as they headed toward the huge grill. Two big coolers full of drinks were next to it, and tables of more drinks and food were next to that. No one would leave hungry today, that was for sure. "It's been weird not having your dad around the last couple weeks."

"No kidding."

Keith Caldwell had recently gotten married to Lana Gonzalez—a woman they all loved—and they'd decided to take a two-week honeymoon to the mountains.

"Maddox is missing him something fierce," Lizzy murmured.

As if he'd realized he was being talked about, her son locked eyes with her, grinned widely, and raced as fast as his little legs would let him go to her. He didn't care who was in his way either, but thankfully everyone made a path for him.

She scooped him up and kissed his cheeks before lifting his shirt and kissing his tummy, making him belly-laugh. He patted her face. "Mama, mama, mama!"

His favorite word for right now. And she would definitely take it. Her own family was cold, so she'd been determined to raise her son differently than she'd been. Surrounded by love, and people who genuinely cherished and cared about them.

She'd sure found that with Porter and his family. And the family they'd created for themselves in the last three years. Blood didn't make someone family, as far as she was concerned.

When Porter wrapped his arms around her and Maddox, pulling them close, she savored the moment. Their little family of three was soon going to be four. She couldn't wait for what the future held.

—THE END—

Dear Readers,

I'm so grateful to all of my readers. And I owe a big thank you to those who have been reading this series from the beginning. If it wasn't for your emails wanting more I might not have gone past book one. I'm so glad I did! This has been such a fun ride and it's hard to believe this is the fifteenth story. Now at the final book, it's a lot more bittersweet saying goodbye to my Red Stone crew than I originally expected. There's always the possibility that one day in the future I'll revisit this world, but for now, it feels done. I'm so happy with the way the series has wrapped up—and I hope you are too. And I really hope you enjoyed the epilogue showing a little glimpse into everyone's lives.

To all my Red Stone readers, thank you for reading this series! Thank you for the reviews you leave, the emails you send and the fun posts on social media I see about this world. You guys are the best and I'm forever grateful for your support.

Best wishes,
Katie

ACKNOWLEDGMENTS

First, I owe a big thanks to the readers of the Red Stone Security series. This series wouldn't have gone as far as it has without you. As always, a big thank you to Kari Walker, quite possibly the biggest supporter of this series! Thank you for reading the early versions of every book. I'm also grateful to Julia for her editing skills, Jaycee for her fabulous cover design, and to Sarah for all the behind-the-scenes work she does that allows me to write more. Thank you to my family for putting up with my writer's schedule! And as always, I'm very grateful to God for so many blessings and opportunities.

COMPLETE BOOKLIST

Red Stone Security Series
No One to Trust
Danger Next Door
Fatal Deception
Miami, Mistletoe & Murder
His to Protect
Breaking Her Rules
Protecting His Witness
Sinful Seduction
Under His Protection
Deadly Fallout
Sworn to Protect
Secret Obsession
Love Thy Enemy
Dangerous Protector
Lethal Game

Deadly Ops Series
Targeted
Bound to Danger
Chasing Danger (novella)
Shattered Duty
Edge of Danger
A Covert Affair

The Serafina: Sin City Series
First Surrender
Sensual Surrender
Sweetest Surrender
Dangerous Surrender

Non-series Romantic Suspense
Running From the Past
Dangerous Secrets
Killer Secrets
Deadly Obsession
Danger in Paradise
His Secret Past
Retribution
Merry Christmas, Baby

Paranormal Romance
Destined Mate
Protector's Mate
A Jaguar's Kiss
Tempting the Jaguar
Enemy Mine
Heart of the Jaguar

Moon Shifter Series
Alpha Instinct
Lover's Instinct (novella)
Primal Possession
Mating Instinct
His Untamed Desire (novella)
Avenger's Heat
Hunter Reborn
Protective Instinct (novella)
Dark Protector
A Mate for Christmas (novella)

Darkness Series
Darkness Awakened
Taste of Darkness
Beyond the Darkness
Hunted by Darkness
Into the Darkness

ABOUT THE AUTHOR

Katie Reus is the *New York Times* and *USA Today* bestselling author of the Red Stone Security series, the Darkness series and the Deadly Ops series. She fell in love with romance at a young age thanks to books she pilfered from her mom's stash. Years later she loves reading romance almost as much as she loves writing it.

However, she didn't always know she wanted to be a writer. After changing majors many times, she finally graduated summa cum laude with a degree in psychology. Not long after that she discovered a new love. Writing. She now spends her days writing dark paranormal romance and sexy romantic suspense.

For more information on Katie please visit her website: www.katiereus.com. Also find her on twitter @katiereus or visit her on facebook at:
www.facebook.com/katiereusauthor.

Made in the USA
Middletown, DE
09 August 2017